RUMOR

To: Mrs. Coleman

Thanks so much for the support! God bless you and yours! I hope you enjoy.

J.E. Tyler

5/15/14

RUMOR

Daughter of Lies

J.E. Tyler

Dedication

I dedicate this book to all the young boys and girls who feel that they are navigating this bumpy road that we call life all alone. You are never alone. God is and always will be walking by your side.

Contents

Acknowledgements

I can't thank God enough for the amazing story that he placed on my heart. Writing this story as a vessel of God's will has been both a humbling and rewarding experience. I also want to thank everyone who has believed in me from day one. If you've glanced upon any of my written words and encouraged me to share it with the world, then this story is definitely for you. I would never have had the courage to share my work on such a public platform without the encouragement of those who love me. Thank you all so much from the bottom of my heart. I also want to thank my parents, James and Cassandra Tyler. You both are my rocks, more so than you will ever realize. I love you and I thank you for everything. To the rest of my family, friends, and the world of supporters; I pray that God blesses every area of your lives. Thanks you!

Chapter 1

Cold World

Most people can't remember the day of their birth, but somehow I can. At least, I seem to think that I can. Maybe it was some sort of dream. I'm not sure, but what I do know is that it was a beautiful day. It was a Sunday morning and the Mississippi sun was as bright as ever; but from the depths of my mother's womb, none of that mattered. It was warm and comfortable inside. I slept to the steady sound of her soothing heartbeat. I was a part of her. Everything was perfect, but then something happened. It was no longer comfortable. My perfect home was now tightening in and around me. I felt restricted. There was an enormous buildup of pressure. It was the most frightening feeling I had ever experienced. I was being forced from my home. I had no idea where I was going. With each passing second, her womb grew tighter. Her heart raced louder. It was only a matter of time before my perfect home ruptured and sent me swimming towards an extremely bright light.

I remember shielding my eyes and screaming for help. I didn't want to see anything. I wanted to return to the warmth of her womb. The hospital room was so cold. Chilly hands gripped me from all sorts of directions. They cut the cord that grew from my navel. I had no idea who they were or what they were doing to me. It was frightening. I was scared out of my mind until I once again felt the warmth of her embrace. I opened my eyes for the first time while lying in her arms. I took sight of her beautiful eyes and wide smile. Those beautiful eyes and that wide smile belonged to the woman I would forever know as my mother, Alieza Arden. She took one look at me and started to sing with the most beautiful voice. The tone of her voice was even more soothing than her incredible heartbeat.

If the truth's gonna hurt,
Then I gotta tell a lie.
I said I'd rather fake a front
Than see a tear in your eye.
Lightening never strikes in the same place twice,
So take your fragile heart,
And put your pain on ice.

It's a cold, cold world,
Be careful who you love, baby girl.
You never know when it's your turn.
Protect your heart or watch it burn.

After she finished her song, I could hear her whisper the name, Rumor. This is what she called me, her Rumor. Within minutes, I returned to sleep. Her arms quickly became my new home. They were a home that I thought I'd never have to leave; but with time, even that would change. Eventually I grew to become a lost and mother—less child. Just as her song so boldly claimed, "It's a very cold world." I am Rumor Arden and this is my story.

"Rumor, wake up chile," a loud yell suddenly consumed my thoughts. That yell belonged to none other than my Aunt HoneyBea. My bedroom door opened as Aunt HoneyBea stood tall in the midst of the

Sunday morning light. Aunt HoneyBea was a woman of large stature, but she was as sweet as honey. Everyone loved Aunt HoneyBea. She was the type of woman who would move the world just to save a simple fly; but just like the bumble bee, Aunt HoneyBea didn't play when it came to her family. Any sign of a threat and she didn't hesitate to show that her sting was mean.

"Dang, Auntie, it's 6 in the morning," my 16-year-old cousin, Gia, who slept on the other side of our bedroom complained while shielding the light of the sun from her eyes.

"Don't sass me, girl. You went to sleep last night without doing them dishes too, so if I were you I wouldn't try me." Aunt HoneyBea snatched Gia's comforter from across her bed.

"It was Rumor's turn to do the dishes. I just got my nails done. They wasn't about to go in no dish water." Gia shot me a dirty look. Gia always acted as if she hated me, but Aunt HoneyBea told me to pay her no mind. She always said Gia loved attention and hated having to share it with any other girl, even her own cousin.

"I ain't ask you whose turn it was. I just spent all morning cleaning this kitchen and cooking these hotcakes. Ya'll better come eat before I get my belt," Aunt HoneyBea warned. Gia rolled her eyes, but she didn't dare speak another word. She knew better than to cross Aunt HoneyBea.

I watched as Aunt HoneyBea stomped out into the hallway and pounded against the basement door.

"Darryl Junior, come up now, boy. It's time for breakfast." Darryl Junior was my other cousin. He was six years older than Gia. Darryl Junior was a smooth talker. He worked as a nightclub promoter in Biloxi. Every night he drove an hour into the city for work and an hour back in the mornings. He couldn't have slept even one hour, but that didn't matter to Aunt HoneyBea. It was Sunday morning and everybody who lived in her house was going to church, regardless.

"Where my sister at?" The ringing of Uncle Champ's keys preceded him as he walked into the front door of the house.

"Champ, don't be tracking that oil on my floor. I just mopped, fool." Aunt HoneyBea gasped as Uncle Champ wobbled into the house. Uncle Champ ran an automobile repair shop out of Aunt HoneyBea's garage. Everyone in our small town of Hurley, Mississippi, used Uncle Champ's shop.

"Sorry bout that Sis, but I could smell your famous hotcakes from out there in that garage. I swear them pancakes the only smell I know that can overpower motor oil." Uncle Champ laughed as his round stomach shuffled with excitement.

"You bet not touch nothing in my kitchen with those nasty hands. Go on back out that door. I'll bring you your breakfast," Aunt HoneyBea exclaimed while shoving Uncle Champ out the front door.

"Hey Uncle Champ." I waved at my uncle before Aunt HoneyBea completely ushered him out the door.

"Mornin' Rumor and Gia," Uncle Champ yelled back through the screen door.

"Yeah, whatever." Gia patted against her freshly relaxed hair while reluctantly heading towards the dining room.

"Any mail from my Mama, Auntie?" I asked Aunt HoneyBea.

"Rumor, you know mail don't run on Sundays," Aunt HoneyBea answered.

"Yea, unlike yo' mama's legs, some places have to close from time to time." Gia spitefully spoke beneath her breathe.

"What you say, girl?" Aunt HoneyBea exclaimed.

"I didn't say anything, Auntie." Gia smiled.

"Gia, don't make me pop you in your fast tail mouth." Aunt HoneyBea put her hand on her hip and pointed the spatula at Gia's head. Gia immediately went quiet. "Rumor, baby, the mail man comes Tuesday morning. You know yo' mama loves you more than anything in this world. Nothing could stop her from getting one of them letters to her baby."

I smiled as Aunt HoneyBea flashed me a look of reassurance.

"Now ya'll finish your breakfast and get ready for church. I'm about to go down in this basement and get your cousin out of that bed," Aunt HoneyBea said while turning her attention towards the basement door. "Darryl Junior, I'm not gon keep telling you to get out that bed, boy."

I could feel Gia's stare burning a hole in the top of my head as she annoyingly tapped her fork against her glass plate. As I looked up from my plate, I could see her face flexing with mischief as she aggressively chewed away at a bite of pancakes. I could only imagine what horrible thoughts were flowing through her hateful mind, but I didn't dare ask. I only lowered my stare back to my plate of freshly cooked breakfast food.

"You do know that Aunt Mildred hasn't eaten, don't you?" Gia continued to add unnecessary tension to the moment by tapping away at her plate of food. "How selfish of you, Rumor. You should take our dear old auntie a plate."

"Why don't you do it?" I said desperately trying to avoid eye contact with my manipulative cousin. Gia knew that I was afraid of Aunt Mildred. This was just another one of her sick attempts to torture me. Aunt Mildred was our oldest aunt. Her mind was ruined by a severe case of Alzheimer's. Advanced osteoporosis combined with a series of debilitating strokes left her disfigured with a hunchback. She was a frightening sight to witness, and I made it my mission to stay out of her presence.

"Really, Rumor? It's Sunday. Are you really going to let our aunt starve on the Lord's Day? What did Pastor Bernard preach last Sunday? Ah, yes, it was love for your fellow man."

"Shut up, Gia. I'm not gonna let you bother me. Aunt HoneyBea will feed Aunt Mildred. She always does."

"Not if she forgot to turn down the fire beneath the hotcakes. It would be such a shame if they burned before our sickly Aunt is able to eat any."

"The stove is off. The pancakes are fine."

"Are they?" Slyly Gia leaned back against her chair and stretched her arms wide as if she was yawning. Without looking, she nudged her fingers against the stove dials, turning the heat to a high temperature.

"Gia, stop. I'm telling Aunt HoneyBea."

"We share a room, Rumor. Aunt HoneyBea can't protect you 24 hours a day, 7 days a week. Tell and I promise I'll make your life hell."

"Why are you so mean?" I cried.

"As far as you're concerned, I'm a saint. Just call me Saint Gia." Gia beamed with satisfaction while watching me squirm uncomfortably. Gia knew that my conscience would get the best of me.

The screech of loose floor boards never seemed so loud before that moment; but as I slowly approached Aunt Mildred's room, each screech sent torrents of fright down my spine. The smell of old cabbage and Bengay filled my nose. I looked down at my hands as they trembled around the plate of hotcakes. I wanted to turn and run so badly; but every time I looked back, I faced Gia's menacing stare.

Hesitantly, I knocked on her door. At first there was no answer. I followed with two more knocks, both more firm than the first, but still there was no answer. "I tried, Gia. She's probably sleep."

"Try again," Gia demanded. I turned my attention from Gia back to the door as it finally swung open.

Aunt Mildred stood before me with her arms spread wide. Her dingy bathrobe flew open beneath her arm span. Her old, wrinkled skin hung loosely from her nude body as she swiftly reached for me. Before I could react, she grabbed my arm and pulled me close to her face. The horrid smell of her breath was indescribable as she screamed, "Knock. Knock. Who's there . . . ? Lies."

My vision blurred with tears as I yelled for dear life. I yanked my arm from her grasp, dropping the plate of hotcakes onto the floor. The glass plate shattered just as I turned wildly running away from Aunt Mildred's bedroom door. Aunt HoneyBea ascended from the basement just in time for me to collide with her bosom. I cried and screamed frantically as she held me closely.

"Rumor, what happened?" Aunt HoneyBea asked as she hugged my trembling body. She then looked up to see Aunt Mildred standing nude in her bedroom doorway. "Mildred, honey, tie up your robe." Aunt HoneyBea pulled me aside, raced towards Aunt Mildred over broken glass, and closed the bedroom door behind them.

I dropped to the floor just across from the basement door as Darryl Junior's shadow stretched across me. "What's going on up here?" Darryl Junior asked, first looking down at me then over towards Gia.

"Beats me. You better get some of these pancakes. They're the bomb. Mmm, mmm good." Gia pretended to be innocent while stuffing her face with hotcakes.

Only my mother's embrace could provide me with the comfort that I needed, so outside on the front porch steps, I sat silently facing the sun. My hair was freshly braided into one of Aunt HoneyBea's signature designs. I wore my favorite dress, a white satin floral gown with a silk bow around the waist. It was a hand-me-down from my mother's teen years. Wearing it always made me feel like she was with me. The warm rays of the sun dried my tears as if my mother was wiping them herself. It was very reminiscent of the moment in which she left. I was only four years old at that time. Tears streamed endlessly down my face as I watched her standing with a large duffle bag in hand. Aunt HoneyBea held me tightly while I fought to join her. My mother stood, staring back at me as the sunlight illuminated her frame through the opened doorway. A single tear escaped her right eye. She cupped her mouth with her free hand as her entire face frowned with pain.

"Mommy, please don't leave me." I remember crying desperately.

"I'll come back for you, baby. I promise God will see us through this."

"Mama."

"HoneyBea, please take care of my baby." My mother sobbed before turning and fading into the sun's rays. I cried and reached for her but she was already gone.

All I had left of her was my satin gown and the Sunday morning sunlight.

"You feeling better, Cuzzen?" Darryl Junior joined me on the front porch steps. Darryl Junior was like the big brother I never had. He provided the perfect balance to Gia's hatred.

"Yeah, I'm okay."

"You do know your mother's coming back for you, right?" Darryl Junior put his arm around my shoulders and watched me with the most easing pair of eyes.

"It's been eight years. Every day is a struggle just to remember her. I don't know, Darryl Junior. I'm starting to think I should just let her go."

"Don't ever let her go. My mother is dead. I miss her so much and Gia never even got a chance to know her. Not only is your mother alive, but she's in Africa doing missionary work. She's dedicated her life to helping little boys and girls just like you to survive. You should be proud."

"But I'm not proud. I know it's selfish, but why can't their mother's help them. I want my mama, Darryl Junior. I need her."

"I know, Cuz. Do you trust me?"

"You know I do."

"Then believe me when I tell you. I can feel it. She'll be back a lot sooner than you think."

"Thank you Darryl. I love you."

"I love you too, Rumor," Darryl Junior said before hugging me.

"Why ya'll out here sitting around? Darryl Junior, I told you to go start that car. Rumor, baby, get up off that dirty step with that pretty white dress on, and Gia come out that house, girl," Aunt HoneyBea fussed while racing for the car.

"I'm curling my hair," Gia yelled.

"If you don't come out that house, I'm gon curl your behind," Aunt HoneyBea threatened while cranking her Cadillac. Darryl Junior and I hopped in the car as Gia ran out of the house with a head full of curlers.

Looking out of the backseat window at the wooded area surrounding the quiet Mississippi roads evoked memories of so many morning rides with my mother. Alieza and I would cruise up and down Interstate 10 with no real destination in mind. She loved the blowing wind that accompanied a morning ride. She would wear her hair down so that it flowed freely with the breeze. I recalled watching her as she harmonized with the tunes of the radio. She was an old school rhythm and blues fan. Whitney Houston, Chaka Kahn, and Donna Summers belted memorable tunes from the speakers. She would glance over at me while pulling back at her wildly blowing hair. I remember looking up at her with the most adoring eyes. She would flash the most beautiful smile; and then with one hand steadying the wheel, she would tickle my side as I giggled with excitement. The road ahead of us would seem so endless, but within my mother's car, none of that mattered. As long as we were together, we proudly anticipated whatever adventure awaited us.

She was such a fun loving woman. Her actions were almost child-like as she mashed heavily upon the gas begging for stronger gusts of wind to enter the car. We both laughed as the road around us melted into a blur of what was once black top and yellow paint. Red and blue lights swirled into view covering us completely. The vision of my mother dancing amidst the lights like the disco queen, Donna Summer, filled me with so much elation, but the imaginary festivities came to an abrupt halt as I realized Aunt HoneyBea was being trailed by a police car.

"Rumor, chile, put on that seat belt," Aunt HoneyBea yelled as I realized the police lights were not just a figment of my memories, but actually current happenings. I scrambled to get into my seatbelt as Aunt HoneyBea quickly parked the car along the side of the road.

"You've got to be kidding me. Does the whole world have to see me with these damn curlers in my head?" Gia quickly attempted to pull the curlers free of her hair as the police car came to a stop behind us. As I looked forward into the rear view mirror, I quickly realized why Gia was in such a panic. It was Deputy Ron Mack, the son of Sheriff Mack, and the brother of Gia's boyfriend local rapper, K Mack.

"Lil girl, if you curse one more word on the Lord's Day, I will slap you in your mouth so help me God." Aunt HoneyBea turned to face Gia.

"Everybody calm down. I got this. Just let me do all of the talking, Auntie," Darryl Junior whispered as Deputy Ron Mack stepped to the passenger door window.

"You know why I pulled you over, Ma'am?" Deputy Ron Mack peered over his shades as Darryl Junior lowered the window.

"Ma'am? Ronald Mack, don't act like you don't know me boy. I'm the one who slapped your lil ashy booty the day you were born back when I used to mid-wife for this town. Now I was doing 45 in a 50. Please tell me why you making me late for church before I get upset." Aunt HoneyBea said completely ignoring Darryl Junior's plea to let him handle the situation. Aunt HoneyBea wasn't the sit—back-and –observe type of woman. She was used to being in control of every situation.

"My apologies, Miss HoneyBea. I was just trying to keep it professional. Papa Mack's kinda coming down hard on the deputies since we're facing a new election and all. You know how that can be. I just wanted to let you know you've got a busted tail light. You may wanna get that fixed. You can never be too careful, especially with your beautiful granddaughters in the back." Ron Mack slyly smiled and winked at Gia as she successfully removed the last curler from her head.

"Well, thank you baby. Now if you'll excuse me, we really are late for church. Why don't you and your daddy come by the house later for some of my famous cobbler? I'm cooking after church." Aunt HoneyBea smiled with her sweet southern charm.

"I think I'll take you up on that Miss HoneyBea. Ya'll be careful out here and say a lil prayer for me in church," Ron Mack said while still shooting a series of flirtatious glances at Gia. He was very smooth with it. If I hadn't been in the backseat alongside Gia with a perfect view of her googly eyes, I would've never noticed the deputy's flirtations with my underage cousin. Clearly Aunt HoneyBea and Darryl Junior had missed the flirting, because Aunt HoneyBea barely tolerated Gia dating K Mack let alone his adult brother.

"Bye Ron." Gia gushed as Ron Mack returned to his police cruiser.

"Bye Ron? What was that?" Darryl Junior inquired.

"Mind your business. I'm just being polite." Gia snapped.

"Save that polite talk for somebody who don't know your mean a—" Darryl Junior quickly caught his tongue at the sight of HoneyBea rolling her eyes in his direction.

"I want the both of you to shut up. I'm making all three of you go up for alter call today. I don't know where you chillen get all that fowl talk from." Aunt HoneyBea fussed non-stop for the rest of the ride to church.

We were very late for church. As we walked into the front doors of the sanctuary, the praises of the gospel met our ears with the banging of the drums. As usual, my attention immediately went to the many church lady hats bobbing back and forth on the heads of the church women. They were always so elaborately styled that even now I think there was some sort of competition and I missed the memo. People shouted and raced up and down the aisles and in between the pews. The choir sang and danced as Deacon Hamilton directed them excitedly. He threw his hands up and down. As if he were a puppeteer, they followed his commands exactly. I stuck close to Aunt HoneyBea as we made our way up to our usual spot in the second pew. Aunt HoneyBea was taken aback to see Sister Emmagene and her family peacefully clapping while sitting in our usual spot. The irritation on my Aunt's face could be seen from across the sanctuary.

"Sister HoneyBea, why don't you all follow me. I saved the perfect seat for you and your family," Sister Janice, the head usher, quickly intervened. Aunt HoneyBea stared at Sister Emmagene with eyes so mean I was surprised she didn't burn a hole in her head; but being the woman of God that she was, she quietly followed Sister Janice to our new seats. Sister Emmagene turned and waived at us as we took our seats towards the back of the church.

"That woman is working my nerves this morning. Lord, please, bridle my tongue," Aunt HoneyBea gasped. She tipped her own church hat to one side completely blocking the sight of Sister Emmagene as she stood to join in praise and worship.

Within five minutes of us sitting down Darryl Junior leaned back and fell asleep. Gia secretly texted her boyfriend, K Mack; and I stood to lean against Aunt HoneyBea's hip as she swayed with the rhythm of the music. As praise and worship concluded Pastor Bernard Johnson and First Lady Silvia Johnson walked out to the church's applause. They walked in the sanctuary with their routine entrance, waving and smiling at the people of the church. Pastor Bernard walked First Lady Silvia to her seat in the front row and then made his way up to the podium to preach.

Before Pastor Bernard could utter one word, Sister Mary Gibson screamed, "Halleluah." She stood in a pair of the highest heels I'd ever seen and leapt into the air. Sister Gibson leapt twice more before twirling and waving her hands wildly. She jerked back and forth as the deacons stumbled to catch her, but every time it seemed she was falling she would jerk forward and continue to dance. Sister Gibson could always be depended on to provide a good show. Her performances were always overtly dramatic and poorly timed. I nearly burst out with laughter when she swung and slapped poor Deacon Booker in the back of his balding head; but when she finally fell out and her mini-skirt flew backwards over her waist revealing a small white thong, I could've cried.

Sister Janice raced up the aisles of the church so fast, I could've sworn she was Jackie Owens himself. The deacons were all wide eyed as they stood speechless staring at Sister Gibson's "unmentionables." First Lady Silvia immediately rose and eyed Pastor Bernard with a look so stern that his dark brown face flushed slightly red. Sister Janice then covered Sister Gibson with silk cloth temporarily ending the morning's spectacle. First Lady Silvia tugged on the hems of her pant suit attempting to regain her self-righteous composure before returning to her seat. I glanced up at Aunt HoneyBea as she shook her head from side to side acknowledging the ridiculous situation. Aunt HoneyBea always said, "Anything and everything you need can be found in the church" and that morning in particular, the church was everything.

"Let Him use you, Sister Gibson. God is moving in this house today," Pastor Bernard shouted, demanding the attention of the congregation. "I don't think ya'll hear me. God is moving in this house today. Can I get an Amen?"

"AMEN," the church shouted as Brother Willie Douglass chimed in on the organ.

"See, I still don't think you heard me, church. The Lord said upon this rock I will build my church; and the gates of hell shall not prevail against it. Can I get an Amen, church?" Pastor Bernard quoted the Bible.

"AMEN," the church shouted again as Brother Malcolm Sanders added the beat of the drums.

Within a matter of minutes, Pastor Bernard had successfully gained the attention of the entire congregation. It was as if Sister Gibson's peep show never occurred. Pastor Bernard was a charismatic speaker and he gave off a vibe that could brighten the darkest day. I could think of no words to describe his magnetism. Aunt HoneyBea always said it was the Lord's anointing. Whatever it was, the man was amazing. Sunday after Sunday I watched with admiration as he astounded the church. I could sit and listen to him speak all day. He was the only person who could demand my attention even half as much as the memories of my mother.

After the church service concluded and the offering baskets were full, the afternoon sunlight dimmed beneath the weight of the clouds. "This old hip is hurting. Rain is coming. Darryl Junior, baby, gon' pull up the car for your dear old Auntie." Aunt HoneyBea's hip was better than any news forecaster.

"Beatrice, honey, when are you goin' to come by the shop. My beauticians can do wonders for you, girl." Sister Emmagene glided towards my Aunt as we were leaving church. Sister Emmagene ran Imagene Beauty, the largest beauty shop in Hurley, Mississippi. Her clients always left styled to perfection even though she often looked like a circus clown. Aunt HoneyBea always said that Sister Emmagene wore her make up so thick that airplane pilots could land planes with just the sight of her blush.

"It's HoneyBea, Sister Emmagene, and as much as I would love to chat, I've gotta get home and get started on my collard greens." I could barely hear Aunt HoneyBea speak as the loud roar of rap music filled the air. We all turned to see a lime green and yellow old model Monte Carlo on 22 inch rims.

"Lil' hoodlums. You'd think their mothers would teach 'em to respect the church. Ugh. I'd just die if one of my daughters brought something like that home." Sister Emmagene curled up her nose into a stink face at the sight of the flamboyantly designed automobile.

Before Aunt HoneyBea could comment, she noticed Gia running to lean against the passenger side window of the car. "Sister Beatrice, isn't that your niece?"

"It's HoneyBea." Aunt HoneyBea fumed as she watched Gia converse with the car's passenger. "Rumor, go get your fast tail cousin before I burn a hole in her behind out here in front of this church."

Before I could even budge an inch, the boy hopped out of the car and hugged Gia tightly. By the sight of his nappy short corn rows, low hanging baggy pants, and the array of unnecessary tattoo art that covered his dark skin, I immediately knew it was Gia's boyfriend K Mack. K Mack and Gia walked hand in hand towards us. I watched as Aunt HoneyBea breathed deeply, anticipating the confrontation.

"Hey, Aunt HoneyBea." K Mack grinned exhibiting a row of golden teeth.

"Lil Boy, I am not your aunt. If I were, I'd beat those braids off you for coming to this church with your pants hanging below your waist like that," Aunt HoneyBea scolded.

"No disrespect, ma. That's just my swag." K Mack grabbed the crotch of his pants and pulled them up as they again drooped beneath his thighs.

"Gia, take Rumor and go get in the car with your brother," Aunt HoneyBea commanded without removing her contempt filled stare from K Mack.

"Auntie, I'm gonna ride back with K Mack. I'll be home later." Gia flashed a false, innocent smile.

"You goin' where? With who?" Aunt HoneyBea screamed.

"Well, Beatrice, I've gotta go find my daughters. Too many thugs on the church grounds this morning." Sister Emmagene rolled her eyes with disgust before turning to leave.

"It's HoneyBea," Aunt HoneyBea raged, still without removing her stare from K Mack.

"Ay Gi Gi, talk to your aunt. I'll be in the G ride with my boy, Toomp." K Mack kissed Gia on the cheek before firmly groping her butt. Aunt HoneyBea's face flushed blood red. At that point if looks could kill, K Mack's obituary would've already been printed in bold type ink.

"Ok, Boo." Gia giggled as K Mack wobbled back towards the Monte Carlo.

"Gia Chantelle Arden, I know you done lost your mind parading that lil' gangsta in front of the Lord's house like some lil' hoe with no home training." Aunt HoneyBea fumed with anger.

"Auntie, he's a good guy. He just pretends to be hard. He's on the honor roll at school."

"Good for him and his mammy, but I'll tell you where he won't be," Aunt HoneyBea continued.

"Where?" Gia asked.

"On my niece."

"Ugh. Why are you trippin? That's my boyfriend."

"Lil girl, question me one more time and you will be riding back home with my high heel in your behind."

"He's a musician, Aunt HoneyBea. He's playing his first gig, tonight. I just wanna support him."

"Gia, I've said all I'm gon' say about it." Aunt HoneyBea spoke with a stern but calm voice that sent chills up my spine.

The loud beep of a car horn blasted from the extravagant Monte Carlo. "Ay, Bae, you coming or not? Ladies free before 10 tonight at the Cabana."

"The Cabana?" Aunt HoneyBea exclaimed.

"Yea. It's this cool teen spot downtown," Gia said with hesitant hope that Aunt HoneyBea would change her mind.

"I didn't know that was a teen spot. Maybe I can go too. I'll ride with Darryl Junior. I know he works there some nights." I beamed with excitement.

"Is that right? Darryl Junior works there, huh?" Aunt HoneyBea asked.

"Shut up, Rumor. Auntie, she don't know what she talking bout. Darryl Junior ain't never been to the Cabana." Gia's words were quickly accompanied by the low hum of Aunt HoneyBea's car as Darryl Junior pulled up.

"What about the Cabana? Ohhh. That's right. That reminds me. Auntie, I'm working tonight. We're promoting some amateur rap concert at the Cabana." Darryl Junior spoke through the rolled down window of Aunt HoneyBea's car.

"The Cabana in Biloxi, right?" Aunt HoneyBea asked Darryl Junior. Gia frantically waived her arms signaling for Darryl Junior to say no, but he never glanced at her once.

"Yeah, Auntie. You know I only work in Biloxi."

"Gia, get in the car, now. Me, you, and my belt will have a long conversation later about your lying." As Aunt HoneyBea spoke a flash of lightening filled the sky. Within seconds, rain fell from the clouds. Aunt HoneyBea's fiery anger was so boldly evident upon her face, that each raindrop met her head with vapors of steam. The ride home was the most quiet I ever remembered it being. Gia's eyes sent threatening signals to me the entire trip.

The best part of Sundays has always been dinner. In a matter of hours, Aunt HoneyBea had concocted perfection from within the walls of her kitchen. The delicious aroma of macaroni and cheese, pork chops, collard greens, black eyed peas, corn bread, gravy, pecan pie, and Auntie's famous peach cobbler flowed throughout the house. Everyone's stomach was on fire with hunger. Our house was filled with guests who couldn't wait to savor auntie's food. Pastor Bernard and First Lady Silvia walked in to join the festivities just as Aunt HoneyBea pulled the cornbread from the oven fully completing her meal. As usual, Pastor Bernard wore the hugest, most handsome smile I had ever seen on a man. His dark brown skin glowed as he stepped into the dimmed lights of auntie's living room.

"Lucky, is that you?" Uncle Champ rushed Pastor Bernard with a half hug, half handshake.

"Champ, I ain't seen you in years. That's hard to do in a small town like Hurley," Pastor Bernard spoke.

"Well, you know you a big time reverend, now. You don't come down here in the boonies with us poor folk, no more," Uncle Champ jokingly replied.

"Oh now Champ, you know that ain't the case. When the last time you been to church, old friend?"

"Well Reverend, it's been nice catching up. I gotta get out here and finish Ms. Minnie's carburetor."

"Yeah, I bet you do." Pastor Bernard chuckled.

"Champ, leave Pastor alone. Don't be in here choking my guests with the smell of all that motor oil." Aunt HoneyBea stepped from the kitchen.

"HoneyBea, you left church in such a rush that we didn't get to speak to you this morning." First Lady Silvia smiled at the sight of Aunt HoneyBea.

"Oh chile, you know how it is round here. These mouths ain't feeding themselves." Aunt HoneyBea snickered while greeting First Lady Silvia with a hug.

"Oh old Champ ain't never a bother. I'm tryna see what I gotta do to get my old friend in church next Sunday." Pastor Bernard smiled while hugging Aunt HoneyBea.

"Pastor, unless we switching to Malt Liquor and fried catfish for communion, I wouldn't hold my breath." Aunt HoneyBea playfully teased Uncle Champ.

"Alright then, Reverend. Don't forget my plate, HoneyBea." Uncle Champ quickly ran from the pressure of church talk.

"That man ain't changed since high school," Pastor Bernard laughed. "Now where is Miss Rumor?"

I sped into the living room and leapt into Pastor Bernard's arms. For some reason, the smell of his cologne always reminded me of my mother. Mama always said Pastor Bernard was a great man. His work within the community was unparalleled. You could definitely feel that he was a true man of God.

"Good evening Rumor." First Lady Silvia stooped low and barely patted me on the head. I never understood why, but she always seemed so uneasy whenever I was around. As she rose back to the elevated height provided by her extra high heels, the glisten of a small, black, cat-shaped diamond tucked away beneath her blouse, caught my eye.

"I got a surprise for you, Rumor," Pastor Bernard said as I pulled my stare away from First Lady Silvia's unusual jewelry.

"Yay. Can I have it now?" I squealed with excitement.

"Well, your auntie tells me you've taken a liking to writing poetry. You know your mother is a poet. She's the best architect of words I've ever met," Pastor Bernard continued.

"Best is such a strong word." First Lady Silvia folded her arms and frowned.

"Silvia," Pastor Bernard said nudging his wife.

"Yes. Best is such a strong word that it definitely exemplifies a strong woman like your mother. The church is so proud of her missionary work in Africa." First Lady Silvia quickly smiled to correct her sour demeanor.

"Exactly." Pastor Bernard reached into his coat pocket and pulled out a small book. "This is a journal, Rumor. I know that mind of yours is filled with so many brilliant words and thoughts, and I know sometimes that it's so hard projecting that brilliance without the guidance of your mother. She's in you though, Rumor. I read some of your poetry. Your auntie brought it to me. It's as if your words are straight from the heart of your mother. They are proof that she is in you. Write them down and keep them close to your heart. I mean real close to the same place that you keep your mother. That way she will feel each word herself as she sits beneath that hot African sun thinking of her beautiful Rumor."

"Thank you, Pastor." I grabbed the journal and again hugged him tightly. He was right. She was in me and I felt her presence every day.

That moment of love was soon interrupted by the presence of hatred. I turned from Pastor Bernard's embrace as I felt a cold, menacing stare across my back. I turned to face Gia. Her eyes were swollen and red from hours of crying. "Really? I'm so sick and tired of everyone pretending that she is so damn perfect all the time."

"Gia, lil girl, don't start no mess in my house. Not today," Aunt HoneyBea yelled.

"Oh no, Gia, don't start no mess. Don't put any holes in our perfect little picture of lies. No, don't do that Gia.

We're a bunch of hypocrites and we wouldn't dare have you expose that," Gia sarcastically rambled.

"Gia, calm down," Pastor Bernard urged.

"I am calm, Pastor. I'm finally calm, because I know that my soul won't burn for this lie. I may be rude, nasty, and downright mean as hell, but with me people know what they're getting. I don't front for anyone, but everyone wants to make me the big bad wolf when I'm simply telling the truth."

"Gia, go to your room, now," Aunt HoneyBea commanded.

"Rumor, your mother's not in Africa doing missionary work. She was the whore of Hurley and she left you for big city men and fatter pockets to pick. She isn't some angel the way they want you to think. It's all a lie. Your mother is a slutty, whoring lie."

Gia's words hit my heart with overwhelming pain. My pupils dilated to the size of boulders as tears fell free from my eyes. The room around me went silent. All eyes were on me and I could see their mouths moving. I could see the expressions of pity in their eyes, but I could not hear a word. There was just the ringing in my ears. The loud ringing of anguish filled my mind. A large lump of nerves filled my stomach. The emotions were too much. I couldn't help but believe Gia. In that moment, I knew that she was speaking the truth. A part of me always knew my mother was a lie, but the most of me never wanted to accept it.

I screamed. I screamed so loudly that I hoped she could hear me. In whatever down trodden corner of shame my mother occupied, I prayed that she could hear me. I wanted her to know my pain. I wanted her to feel the hurt of her neglected daughter. How could she lie to me, her only daughter? She said God would see us through it all. I guess that sentiment never included her own lies.

The thoughts of betrayal were too much for my young mind to grasp. I ran past Gia, pushing her aside as I swiftly raced into our bedroom. I closed the door quickly locking it behind me. I continued to scream as I rushed across Gia's dresser. I threw all of her make-up, her clothes, her hair pins and her scrunchies, her stuffed animals, and everything onto the floor. I grabbed her mirror from her vanity and smashed it into the floor. Broken glass and blood were everywhere as I continued on a rampage across our bedroom. I yanked each of her drawers from the dresser and flung them into the walls. The drawers crashed with loud bangs causing huge holes in the drywall. I then fell to my hands and knees and wept uncontrollably. As I cried, I looked down at something that had fallen from Gia's dresser drawer. It was a pregnancy test. The strip was freshly wet with urine and the sight of the small plus sign brought me to the realization that Gia was pregnant.

Rumor's Journal (Entry 1)

I am but a fabrication,
the full blown daughter of a lie.
I can no longer deny,
No more than I can deny the bold melanin of my
pigmentation.
I am confusion, I am regret,
and I am the makings of a tumor.
I am the mark of shame,
no wonder she named me . . . Rumor.

Chapter 2

A World of Wonder

Some nights I dream about going away to Biloxi with Darryl Junior. His stories of the city make it appear to be a place of magic. There is the way the massive casino buildings cast lights of beauty across the glistening shores of the Gulf Coast. Those bright, colorful lights dance across the waters illuminating it into a sight of fantasy. Then there's the constant ringing of registers as unlimited amounts of cash are exchanged for tiny tokens. The streets are littered with people overjoyed by the sights of these tokens. Exotic and tasty drinks are mixed with potions of liquid joy and freely dispensed to the masses as they excitedly participate in numerous games for prizes of more tokens. There are giveaways of luxury vehicles, jewelry, designer clothing, and any material wish the mind could ever wonder upon. These things make my mind wonder of a world greater than the small town of Hurley, but unfortunately the grandeur of Biloxi is more than a twelve-year-old girl can handle. Well, at least that's what Aunt HoneyBea always tells me. So some nights my imagination takes me away as my cousin's company on his many nights of adventure.

That Sunday night in particular not even my wild imagination could ponder the events of Darryl Junior's night. At home in Hurley, my cousin was Darryl Junior; but in Biloxi Darryl Junior was DJ the Spade, the most valuable piece of a deck of cards. DJ stood tall against the head of a craps table as a formidable opponent to any stickman the Casinos had to offer. His face was always lifted into the most cunning and clever smile. There was no need for a poker face when true skill was left unmatched and DJ was definitely more skilled than most. He held skills that were not limited to just the craps table. He could uncover the mystery of a deck of cards just by looking into the eyes of his opponent, making a difficult game of poker appear to be a simple walk in the park. DJ inherited these skills honestly from our late uncle, Tony P.

Tony P was Aunt HoneyBea's husband. It's always said that it's not wise to speak unfavorable of the dead, but to be honest, Tony P was a drunken gambler with the fowl mouth of a serpent. His miserable nature was definitely the salt to Aunt HoneyBea's sweet sugar. I'd be lying if I said I missed the man. I hated hearing Aunt HoneyBea's sobs after his wild drunken nights of gambling or having to witness the swelling of sorrow that grew over her face after she had to refinance her home in order to pay off his gambling debts. The man was a pariah to our home, but his knowledge of casino gambling always inspired Darryl Junior. Aunt HoneyBea would flip her wig with rage if she knew that Tony P taught Darryl Junior how to gamble. Every day as she left to work, Tony P would engage Darryl Junior in a challenge of wits. Over the years Darryl Junior grew to be even better than Tony P himself. I can even remember the morning Tony P took his last breath. Alcohol abuse had left his liver ridden with cancer. His normally reddish brown skin had transitioned to a sickly yellow complexion. He heaved and coughed for months growing weaker with each day; but on that last day, Tony P smiled just a little bit brighter than usual. He didn't want to see anyone but Darryl Junior. Aunt HoneyBea had no idea why, but she was so happy to see his crooked smile that she happily obliged. That morning Tony P and Darryl Junior engaged in their final poker match. In a way, I think it was Tony P's way of passing his responsibilities as man of the house to my cousin. After an hour long match of stares, Darryl Junior left triumphant and Tony P happily gave his last breath. On that day, DJ the Spade was born.

The biggest difference between Tony P and Darryl Junior had to be Darryl Junior's ambition. Darryl Junior held restraint with his winnings. He would not allow the thrill of the game to overcome him. He knew when to pull back; so instead of losing his tokens to the casino, Darryl Junior used them to fund his own endeavors. He united a team of aggressive promoters to dominate the Biloxi nightlife under the business umbrella of his company, D Spade Promotions.

With the dice rolling back and forth within his right fist, Darryl Junior saw the craps table as a board of angles rather than the highly decorated table that lay before him. The table was surrounded with other people eager to bet their money on Darryl Junior's dice roll. The pressure was thick as Darryl Junior stood facing off against the table stickman in a bet that could potentially break the house.

"Roll the dice, handsome. Mama needs to add a few more cup sizes." Olivia Wright's huge breast implants jiggled within her low cut cocktail dress. Olivia was a regular within Biloxi casinos. She was a beautiful, long legged, busty blonde with a ferocious appetite for powerful men. She had completely run through Mississippi's elite, but Darryl Junior had not yet fallen prey to her feminine wiles. The fact that my cousin was able to elude Olivia, only made her want him more; and she was more than willing to stack the table with poker chips in order to gain his favor.

"Yea, Spade. You scared or something? Roll the dice." A new young casino stickman, Ray, taunted my cousin from the other end of the table. Ray had heard of Darryl Junior's skill on the craps table, but he'd never fallen victim to it. Ray was good at getting into the minds of players and mentally leaving them unable to toss effectively. Because of this, everyone avoided the young man's table, but Darryl Junior was eager for the challenge.

"Spade? Scared? This man ain't heard the word on the streets, I see. We run Biloxi, punk." Red, Darryl Junior's childhood best friend and his right hand promoter within D Spade Promotions, bragged.

"You ran Biloxi, because today is Ray day; and on Ray day, even the best players gotta pay," Ray continued to taunt.

"Put this kid's mouth to sleep, DJ. I've been waiting for this. The little punk took my rent money last week." Earl, a drunken middle-aged man, who was also a casino regular yelled across the table.

"That's right. I took your money last week and looks like I'm about to take the rest of it today. Ya'll trust all of ya'll money to some country boy from Nowhere, Mississippi, who rides out to Biloxi to play king every night. I see through you, Spade. You're just a lil boy getting his rocks off tryna play the part of a man." Ray laughed. The rest of the table nervously watched Darryl Junior as he quietly faced the craps table.

"You know what? You're right, Ray. I'm nothing more than a boy tryna play like a man." Darryl Junior finally spoke.

"Ay, man, what is you saying?" Red barked with confusion at Darryl Junior's words.

"This is the great Spade? Man, I feel cheated. Yo, Olivia, when I finish taking this fool's money, I'ma roll them double D's across this craps table a few times, myself." Ray flashed a mischievous smile showcasing a shiny pair of golden front teeth.

"Please, boy. You can't afford a chick like me." Olivia rolled her eyes while rubbing her fingers through her hair.

"Oh really. Wanna bet on it. I'll take that fly looking black cat diamond you sporting on your finger, mommy." Ray continued to tease Olivia but she simply ignored him while covering her rings beneath the palm of her other hand.

"Ray, you didn't let me finish." Darryl Junior interjected.

"Oh, my bad. I didn't realize that the cat let go of your tongue." Ray laughed.

"No matter what game this boy plays, this boys plays to win. So when I play like a man, you better believe the boy in me gets it in." Darryl Junior closed his eyes briefly envisioning the hard, wrinkled hand of Tony P tossing the dice. "Check em, fool."

Effortlessly, Darryl Junior tossed the dice. Everyone's eyes followed the small, white cubes as they skipped across the green surface of the table. The dice bounced against the wall and rotated backwards, slowly rolling and teasing the table with the thin line between victory and defeat. There seemed to be no sound around the table as the dice finally rolled to a halt. Ray's smiling cheeks froze then fell with bitter disappointment as the dice revealed, "Seven, Eleven."

"That's my dawg," Red shouted with elation as the table erupted into applause.

"Let's get out of here, Red. We got grown man business to handle downstairs in the club," Darryl Junior smirked before tossing one casino chip in Ray's direction. "Buy yourself a drink, boy." Ray caught the chip in hand and clinched it tightly with silent anger.

"Yea, man. About this concert, you sure this kid can flow? I mean I know he's a little legend in Hurley but people around here ain't tryna hear that small town rap," Red said as he and Darryl Junior quickly walked through the casino.

"Red, man, I don't even like this dude. He been sneaking around with my lil sister, but talent is talent. The boy is the truth. I'm tryna get my people outta Hurley, bruh. These lil parties make good money, but cats is out here making good lute in this rap game. This is how we're going to put D Spade Promotions on the map, homie."

"I hear ya, DJ. You know I got your back. I just wanna make sure you thought about this stuff. The other promoters have been talking."

"Man, let them birds chirp. We gotta squad, don't get me wrong; but them boys don't see the big picture. They're workers, not bosses. I'm on my boss game right now. D Spade is going to the next level by any means necessary."

"My man, Spade. I'm with you. Let's make this money." Red smiled as he and Darryl Junior clasped hands with pride.

As the elevator door opened revealing their path to the nightclub that operated on the casino's second floor, the fragrance of expensive perfume and essential oils captured Darryl Junior's nose. He and Red shot one another a look of agreement, both knowing the source of the sweet aroma. "I'll see you downstairs, bruh," Red smirked before walking onto the elevator alone.

"It smells like the flowers of heaven just rained down on earth. Mmm, a smell that delicious can only be Chrisette Carter." Darryl Junior turned around to lay eyes on the brown skinned beauty with long, dark, silky hair flowing down around her face. Half Native American and African American, Chrisette had the face of an angel but she was as tough as a bull, and the angry look on her face spelled trouble for my cousin.

"Save the sweet talk for one of those dumb hoes out here. I'm not impressed, Darryl Junior," Chrisette snapped.

"C'mon now, Chrisette. You know I go by Spade out here."

"I could care less about whoever you are deciding to be, today. I thought we agreed you and your people were going to stop coming in here breaking my grandfather's casino."

"Chill, girl. I have every intention of giving the money back to Mr. Carter."

"Then why take it in the first place? Why are you even here?"

"I have a reputation to maintain. I can't have your employees in here talking slick about the Spade. I just had to introduce myself to the new stickman. That's all. Plus I'm promoting the rap concert downstairs."

"You are so typical. Always giving a damn about what the next man thinks. That's why you and I would never have worked out." Chrisette crossed her arms and shook her head with disappointment.

"Chrissy, you know you miss me. Why are you still trippin'?"

"Cause you don't get it, Darryl. You never did and I'm tired of trying to explain it to you. I'll talk to the booking department about not clearing this concert with me. But for future references, you nor your janky promotions company are allowed in this casino."

"You know what? That's cool with me, but don't come crying to me when ain't no business coming through this low-budget casino," Darryl Junior snapped in retaliation. Just as Chrisette's eyes tightened with anger and her mouth swelled in preparation to curse Darryl Junior, the walkie-talkie on her waist sounded, breaking the air of frustration surrounding them.

"Yeah." The irritation in Chrisette's voice could be heard over the radio waves as the outside security guard called for her.

"We've got a problem outside." The security guard spoke.

"Then handle it. Isn't that what we pay you for?" Chrisette fumed with anger.

"Yes, Ms. Carter; but this problem says that he knows you. He's saying he's with D Spade Promotions." Darryl Junior's nerves were uneasy as he heard the security guard speak the name of his company.

"Funyun!" Darryl Junior and Chrisette both exclaimed in unison. Funyun was Darryl Junior's other childhood best friend but unlike Red, Funyun was a habitual screw up. Funyun was an overweight ex-football star who lost his college scholarship to Mississippi State University for having sex with a drunken freshman who just happened to be the University President's daughter. Funyun's popularity in Mississippi due to his success in sports made him a perfect addition to D Spade Promotions, but his weakness for food and women made him a never—ending liability that Darryl Junior often paid for.

Chrisette and Darryl Junior stormed out into the cool night air of Biloxi to see an insanely inebriated Funyun surrounded by four barely dressed prostitutes. Three of the four heavily made-up prostitutes were also clearly high as kites, but the face of the fourth woman was out of view as she kneeled down puking in the casino's large water fountain. Darryl Junior quickly grabbed Chrisette's arm before she could proceed on her path of rage toward his friend and the four hookers.

"You've got five minutes before I knuckle up on a few drunk whores. Get them out of here, Darryl," Chrisette screamed.

"Funyun, man, what the hell are you doing bringin' them here," Darryl Junior yelled while approaching his friend.

"Spade, what's poppin with the concert, homie? I want you to meet the girls: Legs, Titties, Ass, and that one over there throwing up in the pool is Beauty. You gotta see her, bruh. She bad." The woman did not turn around as she continued to gag and heave loads of digested food into the casino's fountain.

"You gotta go home, man. I can't let you in here like this." Darryl Junior sighed at the wasted sight of his friend.

"Like what? I'm fine, bruh."

"You're high as hell and your breath smells like hot garbage. Just go home."

"Go home? Funyun, you promised you could get us in. Caesar ain't gon like this," One of the prostitutes slurred over drunken words.

"Spade, look man. I need you to help your boy out with this one," Funyun whispered while pulling Darryl Junior aside and away from the prostitutes. "This pimp named Caesar let me have these hoes for free, tonight. All I had to promise was that I could get them in the concert. He just wants the hoes to meet a few ballers tonight man."

"Take these girls back, man. And get this other one to a hospital or something. That is nasty." Darryl Junior pulled away from Funyun and reached out to pull the woman away from the fountain.

"Hey, man. Get your hands off me," the woman fussed while turning to face Darryl Junior.

"Is there a problem?" Chrisette chimed in more than willing to face off with the woman, but Darryl Junior could not answer her. He was frozen in place as he stood facing a very familiar face.

"It can't be you . . ." Darryl Junior uttered.

"Oh damn," the woman replied before her dizzy eyes rolled backwards into her head as she fainted. Darryl Junior quickly grabbed her, pulling her unconscious body out of the fountain water.

"Darryl Junior, what are you doing? You can't just bring her up in here." Chrisette grew angrier with each passing moment as Darryl Junior raced up towards the fourth floor casino hotel rooms with the unconscious prostitute in his arms. She chased behind screaming at him with each step as they made their way up to the rooms, but Darryl Junior did not acknowledge her. His focus was on the woman in his arms. "Don't make me call the police. Get her out of here."

"Chrissy, she's my family. Please open one of the empty rooms so I can lay her down."

"Your family? What? Who is she?" Chrissy asked.

"This is Alieza, Rumor's mom."

Rumor's Journal (Entry 2)

The night awakened me with whispers of " I wonder,"
I wonder where could she be,
Does she think of me,
Am I in her head,
Or in her heart do thoughts of me lie dead?
I hate her, but still I love her,
It's a bitter irony, void of humor,
I wonder am I her truth or still a false Rumor?

Chapter 3

A Field of Butterflies

Monday morning met me with pain, but the pain in my glass scarred arms was nothing compared to the pain in my heart. My whole life had been a lie told to me by the people I trusted most. I didn't know what to feel; and even if I were ever able to figure it out, the pain had left me completely numb inside. I looked over at Gia still asleep in her bed. She looked so peaceful. I wanted to hate her, but I couldn't. She was the only one who'd ever told me the truth. Gia may have been mean, but she was honest. Strangely, I pitied her more than anything. There was a child growing inside of her, a secret that she endured all alone. Maybe that was the way my mother felt when she discovered that she was pregnant with me. I couldn't help but think that maybe I had been her secret shame. That was why she left me. I couldn't blame her for leaving. I saw the pain in Gia's eyes. Her heart was heavy with the burden of another life. It was a shame that I would never wish on another person, especially not my mother.

Aunt HoneyBea had completely cleaned our bedroom of any sign of my destructive tantrum, but somehow the scene around me still seemed broken. The shadows of tree branches swaying in the wind extended beyond the sunlight growing into our room. Like arms, the shadows reached for me. For a brief moment they were my mother's arms; but as I listened quietly, I could not hear her song. It was the clearest sign that she was lost to me forever.

The only sounds were the sweeping of the wind and the voices from Aunt HoneyBea's television. The weather man spoke of a category one hurricane moving up towards the Gulf of Mexico. They'd named it Veronya. The powerful lashing of strong winds erupted from the television as one newscaster stood off the coast of Cuba. Veronya danced around him, relentlessly blowing him in all directions. He stumbled over his words while attempting to report the storm's impact on Cuba. All sorts of debris floated through the air as the man shielded his face from the angry storm. Large powerful waves washed against the shore. The sight of wrecked boats and ships littered the sandy beaches of the Cuban coast. Not a single soul could be found on the streets as the storm proceeded to inflict immaculate amounts of damage.

"Mildred, look at this fool. Honey, you can't pay me enough to be out there working in no hurricane." Aunt

HoneyBea giggled while pulling a piece of cloth beneath the needle of her sewing machine. When Aunt HoneyBea used her sewing machine, the results were always magic. The things that woman could do with a needle and some thread were enough to puzzle a rocket scientist.

Aunt Mildred sat quietly rocking back and forth in her rocking chair. Her body was immobile beneath the shadows cast within her corner of the room. She murmured something in reply to Aunt HoneyBea's words; but to my ears, it all seemed to be gibberish.

"Yea, you know the drill. They about to get err'body all worked up buying water, flashlights, and what not for this storm that's probably going to die out there in the Gulf somewhere. Chile, these people on this news been sanging that same ol' song for way too long," Aunt HoneyBea said.

Aunt Mildred let out a low, deep groan that lasted for what seemed like minutes. I could only assume it was laughter as Aunt HoneyBea quickly joined her with a light chuckle. Even though Aunt Mildred's speech usually seemed like some sort of foreign language to me, Aunt HoneyBea always understood her perfectly. Many times I would just sit back and observe them as they cackled away like sisters do. In many ways, it humanized my Aunt Mildred. As long as I could remember she'd always been so frightening to me, but when she and Aunt HoneyBea would talk, I could almost see slight remnants of what was once a girlish smile forming across her face.

"Lies." As I hid quietly in the dark hallway outside of Aunt HoneyBea's bedroom, I was caught by surprise when Aunt Mildred's eyes suddenly met my own.

"Mildred, what you talkin' bout honey?" Aunt HoneyBea asked while scanning the hallway herself.

"Lies. Lies. Lies," Aunt Mildred screamed.

"Rumor, chile, is that you in that hallway?" Aunt HoneyBea shouted.

"Yes Ma'am," I quietly spoke before standing into the path of light formed by the television screen.

"Girl, its 4:30 in the morning. What you doing outta bed?"

"I couldn't sleep, Aunty. I'm sorry for yesterday," I uttered softly still startled by Aunt Mildred's stare which was locked heavily upon me.

"Aww, baby, come on over here." Aunt HoneyBea spoke with a warm tone full of love. I slowly stepped into her embrace. Her large arms smothered me with affection as I laid smiling in her bosom. Aunt HoneyBea's hugs were like Tylenol. They were the perfect pain reliever. "You know Aunty loves you, right?"

"Yes Ma'am." I smiled.

"Well, don't you ever forget it. No matter what happens baby, I need you to know that you are loved. The world is going to throw a lot at you, more pain, strife, and heartache than you could ever imagine. If you remember that you have a family that has your back no matter what, you can face anything. That includes the truth of your mother."

"Where is she, Aunty?"

"Only God knows, baby; but the way I see it, that leaves her in the best hands possible. There's no need to worry. God is still in control."

I sat in Aunt HoneyBea's lap with my head lying firmly against her heartbeat; and before I knew it, I was soundly asleep. That night's dream found me flying with the winds of Veronya. With my arms spread wide, I soared across the heavens without a worry in the world.

Hours later I stood before the school yard as the first bell rang. Crowds of preteens raced into the building to find their classrooms. I quickly scanned the school yard for my best friend, Taylor. Seeing Taylor was like a breath of fresh air. We had been best friends since kindergarten when Donald Brown tried to steal Taylor's lunch. Taylor was always a lot smaller than the rest of the boys in school, but he was always so cute to me. His little beady eyes and large round dimples always gave me so much joy, so much that I hated to see him without a smile. Well when Donald Brown snatched Taylor's lunch in kindergarten, Taylor cried like a little baby. I couldn't stand seeing him cry. I grabbed a large Lego block and flung it directly at Donald's head. The block smashed against Donald's head with a direct impact. He fell to his knees and sobbed for help. Somehow, Taylor and I were both thrown into time-out for the remainder of the afternoon, but we laughed endlessly at the sight of Donald Brown's face when that Lego hit his head. We were best friends ever since that day.

"Rumor. Please tell me you did Mr. Falon's homework." As soon as our eyes connected, Taylor raced towards me pulling his backpack from his back.

"Don't tell me you forgot your homework, again? Why didn't you call me yesterday? We got 10 minutes before the tardy bell rings." I said.

"I did call. Pastor Bernard answered. He said you were busy. What was I supposed to say? It's an emergency, man of God? I need to cheat off her homework. Why was the pastor answering your house phone anyway?" Taylor asked.

"It's a long story. Just take this homework and hurry up. You've got five minutes." I instantly shoved the homework in his direction, not wanting to relive the events of yesterday.

Taylor took the worksheet and quickly copied the answers. Taylor never remembered his homework. He'd become so good at copying my answers, that I swear he could've set some sort of speed writing record with the Guinness Book of World Records. We scurried through the crowded hallway of students racing against the clock. Tardiness was automatic detention at Hurley Middle School and no one wanted to sit in detention and watch Ms. Ogre pick her nose for an hour. Ms. Ogre was a bugger flicker and many students had come dangerously close to losing an eye under her watch.

As we ran through the hallway, I noticed that something was strangely different. Usually Taylor and I were invisible to the other students; but for some reason, all stares seemed to be fixated on me. For a second, I convinced myself that it was all in my head until I was completely blindsided by the Tahiri triplets: Tasha, Tami, and Tamika. The Tahiri triplets were the biggest gossipers in the history of Hurley Middle School. The three of them were notorious for instigating fights and spreading defamatory lies about people, but no one would dare to challenge them. The three of them together were like a three—headed dragon. Whenever they opened their mouths to speak and no matter what direction their breaths blew in, pain and destruction always followed.

"Every time I look up, the two of you are together. 'Sup with that?" Tasha stood above me with one eyebrow raised into her forehead.

"Gurl, they runnin' around here bumpin' on the low. They ain't foolin nobody." Tamika rolled her eyes.

"We just tryna get to class before the tardy bell rings. Do ya'll mind moving?" Taylor snapped.

"Unh Unh, you better watch it with all that attitude lil' boy. I am not the one." Tasha retorted.

"Ya'll leave these kids alone. If they wanna do their thang on the low, let them. Shoot. I ain't hating." Tami laughed hysterically.

"Nobody is trying to do anything but get to class on time. Maybe the three of you should try that every now and then. It could only help that tongue-popping speech of yours." Before I could catch myself, the words had already left my mouth. I had sarcastically insulted the Tahiri triplets. The entire hallway filled with "ooh's" and "aah's."

"You think you smart, huh, trick?" Tasha said. "Don't fool yourself. You about as smart as that hoe-ish mammy of yours."

"Yeah. That's right. We know everything and you'd do well to keep your mouth shut, lil trick." Tamika reached out and grabbed me with one arm and swung her fist at me with the other. Taylor jumped in between us and took the force of her blow across his chin. I watched as my best friend dropped to the ground gripping his face in pain.

Rage consumed me as I pushed Tamika backwards into the crowd of spectators. The last thing I remember seeing in that moment was Tasha and Tamika both grabbing me. I swung my arms fiercely as the adrenaline in my body rushed through me with maximum speed. Before I knew it, I had blacked out completely.

The tardy bell rang loudly throughout the hallways as students rushed into their classes. The aching sensation in my knuckles pulled me back to reality. My backpack was ripped in half as my papers and books were everywhere. The tussle with the triplets had disturbed my glass wounds causing me to bleed profusely from my arms. Blood was everywhere. Taylor stood next to me inquiring as to whether or not I was okay, but all I could do was look down at the calamity surrounding me. He and I were the only two left standing in the hallway. The Tahiri triplets had vanished with the rest of the crowd.

"Why are you two not in class? Why is all this mess in the hallway? What happened to your arms, Rumor?" Mr. Falon gasped at the sight before him.

They say that good luck comes in threes; but whoever conjured up that thought, didn't know the Tahiri triplets. After my encounter with the three sisters, I was left alone with my thoughts in the school nurse's office. I sat staring at my freshly wrapped, blood stained bandages knowing that they would forever be my mark of shame. Before Sunday evening, I had always been the daughter of a lie; but with the entire town knowing the truth, I was now the daughter of a pariah. I could hear the whispers of the other kids on the other side of the office door. I had fooled myself into thinking that my life could go on as before. Everything had changed, and it became painfully clear that I would never be the same.

Pools of water flowed from my eyes as my mind rested on a series of depressing thoughts. I looked around at the office around me: the bright colors, smiling animations, fun facts, and all kinds of jovial décor. The sight of it all made me sick to my stomach. My muscles tightened under strained nerves. My mouth watered with the threat of regurgitation. I had reached a very low point and I saw no way out. I wanted my arms to bleed. I wanted them to continue bleeding until there was nothing left of me. I grabbed my wounded arm and squeezed hard. The pain shot from my arms up through my entire body. I squeezed harder as the bandages grew redder. I closed my eyes and prepared for the end.

My eyes suddenly shot open as there was a knock on the office door. After one quick knock, the door opened. "This old man seen plenty of kids. This old man seen plenty of roaches. Kids and roaches. Kids and roaches. They'll eat your food, they'll take your house, leave you filth, both small and sly. Now the only difference between chillen and roaches is simply roaches don't cry." Old man Pete the Janitor came dancing into the office with his mop in hand.

I quickly wiped my eyes and did my best to hide my bleeding arms. After hearing my movements, Pete looked up into my startled eyes and flashed me a puzzled look. "You must be the lil' nugget that bled all over the hallway. What's wrong with you kids and all that messy fighting? I'll tell you what. Back in my day, we knew how to whoop tail without getting blood all over the place."

"I-I-I was just waiting on the nurse to come back." I stuttered.

"Good luck with that. That women ain't stutting you chillen. She too busy sneaking around here with that P.E. coach. Now stay out my way while I mop this floor."

"But won't that make the floor slippery?" I asked.

"Look, child, when I put this lil yellow caution sign on this floor, I could care less who fall and break they neck. This ain't elementary. You chillen should know how to read," Pete said before continuing to whistle his tune of kids and roaches while pushing the sudsy mop across the floor.

"Yeah, I'll just take my chances waiting for the nurse in the hallway."

"Lil girl, I don't care if you wait for that woman in traffic. Just get out my way, nah." Pete fussed while shoving the office door closed behind me.

As I stepped out into the hallway, I was surprised to see that it was empty. There was not one person in sight. Everyone was still in class. I had imagined the whispers from earlier. My paranoia was playing tricks on my mind. The sound of shoes tapping against the floor tiles left me thinking that the mind tricks were just beginning.

"Fighting, Rumor? What has gotten into you, girl?" Aunt HoneyBea came stomping around the corner with her heels tapping roughly against the floor.

"Ms. HoneyBea, have there been any problems around your home, lately? It's not like Rumor to misbehave and we were alarmed to see the cuts on her arms." Principal Davis attempted to keep up with Aunt HoneyBea as she sped towards me. I could feel the anger coming from her.

"Principal Davis, if there are any problems within my home, I hardly think that it's any of your business. Now I will handle Rumor if you'll excuse me."

"As a school official and acting guardian of the child during school hours, problems with the child are my concern." Principal Davis continued, but Aunt HoneyBea shot him a look that would send chills through the sun.

"Mr. Davis, please don't make me act my color in this school today."

"Apologies. I'll let you handle Rumor, but we really should discuss this later." Principal Davis froze mid-step not wanting to further anger Aunt HoneyBea.

"Rumor Arden, I'm gon put so much fire to your tail, you won't be sittin' for weeks." Aunt HoneyBea snatched me up into her furious grip.

"Now Taylor why would you go and get yourself into some trouble? You know your father's been under a lot of pressure since he returned from his deployment." Louise Vazquez, Taylor's mom, came walking down the hallway minutes later with Taylor dragging his feet behind her.

"It wasn't our fault, Ma," Taylor said.

"Well, that's for you and your father to figure out later." Louise quickly pranced past us with thick dark sunglasses covering her eyes. Her long thick hair was spread out over her face as she walked with her head slightly down. As mysterious as Louise appeared, it was the look on Taylor's face that alarmed me. I'd never seen him with so much fear in his eyes. I hoped I hadn't gotten him into too much trouble. Not only was my mother's reputation ruining my life, but now it was causing me to ruin Taylor's. I glanced up at Aunt HoneyBea's disapproving eyes then immediately dropped my head in shame.

After such a horrible morning, the last thing I wanted to do was spend my afternoon around a bunch of old gossiping women, but I found myself downtown at Sister Emmagene's beauty shop anyway. Imagene Beauty stood out among the other ordinarily decorated store front buildings of the Hurley strip mall. A beautifully painted pink and purple sign completely covered the top of the building. The glass front windows were painted with the long lashed eyes of a beauty queen. The inside of the building was equally lavish. The theme of the ambiance was somewhere in between Grecian paradise and ghetto chic. The minute we stepped into the building, my focus was immediately captured by large white pillars wrapped with glittery feather boas. There were white washed walls with a trim of pink and purple crown molding. The ceiling was lined with round, violet light bulbs that cast a series of purple trails across the floor. Even the hair dryers were covered with pink and purple plush material. The sounds of the ocean breeze were mixed with the smooth tunes of Anita Baker and broadcast throughout the shop. I struggled to hold my breath for as long as possible against the thick fumes of hair chemicals dominating the air; but with a throbbing headache forming inside of my head, it became clear that I could not escape the putrid air of the shop.

"Beatrice. What a wonderful surprise? Welcome to Imagene, where true beauty goes beyond your imagination." Sister Emmagene sashayed out into the waiting area to greet us. Her every movement appeared overwhelmingly dramatic as her dress sleeves draped beneath her arms like the wings of a giant bird. "So what can we do for you? I'm imagining a low cut with blonde dye. You're giving me Mary J. Blige, honey. Can you say, what's the 4-1-1?"

"Now, Sister Emmagene, don't get carried away. I just want a perm and a curl. That's it." Aunt HoneyBea said.

"Oh, Beatrice. Child, live a little." Sister Emmagene grabbed Aunt HoneyBea by the arm pulling her further into the beauty parlor.

"It's HoneyBea." I could hear Aunt HoneyBea fussing as she vanished behind thick clouds of hairspray.

With Aunt HoneyBea out of sight, for the first time I really focused on the other women in the shop. I realized that all eyes were fixated on me. "Mmm Hmm that's her girl," one of the hair technicians whispered into her clients ear.

"She looks just like her mama," a heavy set woman with large pink rollers in her head gasped. Almost as if her words were a catalyst, the entire shop seemed to erupt with quiet whispers. Their judgments were loud within my mind. I couldn't take another second of the gossip. I rushed out of the double doors of the shop into the streets of downtown Hurley. I ran through the streets as fast as my short legs would take me.

There was only one place that could calm my nerves. It was a place that had secretly provided Taylor and me a source of comfort and enjoyment for years. During Taylor's father's first Army deployment to Iraq many years ago, our bond as friends deepened while we both dealt with the grief of an absentee parent. Taylor's mother, Louise, soon fell into a deep period of depression leaving Taylor just as much an orphan as I was myself. We would talk for hours about running away to find our parents together. We wished we could fly across the world and easily locate them from the heavens, but unfortunately flight was for the butterfly. That, however, didn't stop us from dreaming. We would run out to a large field in which the grass grew several feet high. Taylor and I called it the field of butterflies. As we raced across the grassy land, the shaking of leaves would cause the butterflies to rise into the air, flapping their bright and beautiful wings in unison. All together they created a gorgeous sight, painting the field with their many elaborate colors. The threat of lurking predators such as snakes and bumble bees seemed non-existent beneath the hypnotizing effects of the butterflies' flight. Through those moments, we soared through endless beauty. We felt untouchable to the tragedies of reality. Later that afternoon as the sun prepared to set across the horizon, I raced the wind through the field of butterflies. It was just as perfect as I remembered it until Aunt HoneyBea eventually caught up with me.

"Rumor Lashalle Arden, I don't know what has gotten into you, lil girl, but you'd better fix it now. And I mean right now." Aunt HoneyBea scolded me through tightly shut teeth. Her eyes were tight with fury. I knew that it was taking everything within her not to knock me unconscious.

"HoneyBea, what you doing out here with all that fuss? You are scaring off my customers." Uncle Champ came rushing out of the garage as Aunt HoneyBea continued to scold me in the front yard. It had taken her hours to find me. She looked everywhere, but only Taylor and I knew of the field of butterflies. Eventually, after my legs grew tired of running through the grassy land, I returned to Imagene Beauty shop where Sister Emmagene immediately called Aunt HoneyBea.

"Not now, Champ," Aunt HoneyBea screamed.

"You mean to tell me you out here fussing at Rumor. That sweet lil girl can do no wrong." Uncle Champ stood with a look of shock on his face.

"Rumor, go inside and I don't wanna hear a peep from you or I will tear your hide three new holes and a nostril. You hear me?" Aunt HoneyBea retorted. I quickly found my way to my bedroom where I buried myself deep beneath my bed sheets and comforter.

"HoneyBea, cut the baby some slack. She misses her mama," Uncle Champ said to Aunt HoneyBea after it was clear that I was out of sight.

"I've been running around Hurley sick to my stomach for the past two hours looking for that child. She is not a baby. She is a young woman, and I will not have her disrespecting my rules under my watch. You got a problem with that." Aunt HoneyBea turned her wrath towards Uncle Champ.

"No Ma'am. Sis, I'm good. I was just saying take it easy on her. That's all." Uncle Champ wisely accepted defeat and returned to his auto repair shop in the garage.

That night as I lay sound asleep in my bed, Taylor's voice whispered its way into my mind. I jumped from my bed to see that it was not a dream. Taylor's sad eyes gazed upon me through my bedroom window. I immediately turned to see that Gia was still asleep. Quietly, I crept out into the hallway, making my way into the windy outside air. "What are you doing out here? Do you know what time it is?"

"I can't take it anymore, Rumor. I just can't." Taylor's voice shook with tears of anxiety. I looked into his face and noticed that his skin was swollen and dark around his left eye.

"Who did this to you?" I gasped.

"We spent so many nights crying about our parents. I remember wanting him to come back home so bad that it hurt, but now that I have him back, I know that there is no pain worse than having him here. He's not the same, Rumor. I don't know what they did to him over there, but he's not the same." Taylor wept uncontrollably.

"What are you talking about? I don't understand."

"You always ask me why I never do my homework anymore. Well, it's kinda hard to finish homework over the sound of your father beating your mother to death every night. Mom says I shouldn't say anything. She says he's just broken by some of the things he saw over there, but she's wrong Rumor. He's more than broken. He's not even the same man. I don't see the man I once knew in his eyes. He's lost. He's dead. Now he's just a shell of booze and drugs."

"Did he do this to your eye?"

Taylor dropped his head and nodded reluctantly. "He wasn't too happy about me getting in trouble today at school."

"Oh my God, Taylor. I'm sorry. I'm so sorry. This is all my fault. I dragged you into my mess. All day I've been complaining about my mother, and here you are silently dealing with something like this. Taylor, I'm sorry."

"It's not your fault, Rumor. It would've happened anyway, eventually. He's lost to us. Be glad your mother has not returned, because once they leave, they bring demons back with them."

"I'm going to get Aunt HoneyBea. She'll make this right. She'll know exactly what to do. She always does."

"No. You can't tell anyone." Taylor exclaimed.

"Why not? He's hurting you."

"I can't do that to my family. It's a secret that we have to carry alone. Please, promise me that you won't say anything, Rumor." Taylor's bruised and swollen eyes shed tears all across his face. He was right. His father wasn't broken, he was. My best friend was broken beyond recognition, and what was worse was the fact that I hadn't even noticed.

"I promise." I cried before gripping Taylor with the firmest hug that I could muster. His body trembled within my arms. I wanted to make it better. I wished I could take at least half of his pain.

As if he could hear my thoughts, Taylor immediately pulled away from me and looked into my face with a slight smile. "Let's fly with the butterflies. Just you and me, Rumor. Let's fly."

The strong winds of that night blew the tall grass of the field roughly against our faces, but Taylor and I did not mind the lashing as we watched the sky illuminate with the beauty of the butterflies. The stars twinkled against their wing spans. Pollen spores danced between them. The hooting of the night owls and the chirping of crickets provided the soundtrack to our beautiful night. We had run through the field of butterflies so many times before, but never at night. It was more glorious at night. It was more intimate and the exhilaration of the moment was way more intense. I heard Taylor laughing as we separated, running loosely through the grass. The sound of his laughter filled me with joy. He was happy and so was I. Our problems were so far beneath us as we flew high with the butterflies.

Just as everything was perfect, the high roar of a motor engine sounded from outside of the fields. Tires screeched and in a moment, Taylor's laughter stopped. The butterflies descended and the stars dimmed. The owls and crickets ceased to sing as an ominous feeling overcame me. I dashed through the fields hurriedly screaming Taylor's name but he didn't answer. High beams caught my eye and I followed them out into the street. Taylor lied stiff against the black top road as his father stood over him screaming for help. Bottles of liquor fell from the opened door of his truck.

"I didn't mean to. He's okay, right? Please tell me he's okay." Taylor's father turned to me with fear and tenderness in his blood shot eyes. "I couldn't see him. He's okay right? Wake up, Taylor. Wake the hell up, boy. Wake up." His voice echoed across the fields and out into the night's air. The strong winds blew his words throughout every section of Hurley. I just stood there speechless at the sight of my literally broken, best friend.

Rumor's Journal (Entry 3)

A lifetime of cracks, dents, and decay,
Fearing too strong of a wind may break me any day
Facing the light, I'm see-through like glass,
But hiding in dark, I create reflections of my past.
Trapped in the lowest of times, how long will this last?
Open mouths always ready to put me on blast.
I cover my ears, but they taunt me more.
I'll never be free, always their rumor.

Chapter 4

The Return of Lies

When a source of light goes out, hopeful eyes are shrouded with the hopeless nature of darkness. For me, too many lights had gone dim. I could not see even a sparkle to guide me through life. My best friend was fighting for his life in intensive care; everyone I loved had lied to me; and my mother existed only as the ghost of their many lies. I couldn't wipe the bloody, unconscious sight of Taylor from my mind. In my head, I could still picture him lying immobile against the asphalt road with his leg twisted and broken into an impossible position beneath him. The severity of the moment burned my nerves. His father's hopeless eyes were already lost to the darkness. He saw no way out of his own misery, so he fled. Taylor's father raced out into the darkness, leaving me to kneel alone facing his son's body. The pressure behind my eyes was massive, but I could not shed a tear. The screams in my thoughts were overwhelming, but I didn't make one sound. The trembling of my bones provided an uneasy sensation, but I did not move. I sat kneeling over Taylor until the red and blue lights of police sirens located us. Aunt HoneyBea scurried through ranks of cop cars and an ambulance to gather me into her embrace. As the familiarity of her scent, fresh baked bread and dove soap, met my nose, I finally unleashed a tear. A single tear dropped down the side of my tired face.

Even though my light had been nearly extinguished, a light even more detrimental to Hurley's hope slowly dimmed into obscurity. There were demons in Pastor Bernard's darkness, demons of his past that he'd avoided for way too long. His mind was betraying him as cracks slowly formed throughout his mask of peace and happiness. Thick clumps of mud spread out over the palms of the Pastor's shaking hands. Dirt dried beneath his fingernails as he panicked to cleanse himself of the filth of regret. He looked up to see a large headstone growing from the swampy grounds beneath him. He slowly backed away as the shadow of the growing tombstone consumed his presence.

"Lord, please, forgive me." Pastor Bernard cried as the headstone stood fully erect as a giant above him. The inscription read, *Alieza Arden both a Mother and a Lie. May She Rest in Peace.*

Pools of tears clouded his vision as he cried for mercy, but the weight of the truth was too much for the pastor. The headstone was a reminder of his past and that it was finally catching up to him. The headstone shifted wildly shaking the ground beneath him. Pastor Bernard fell to his knees. The wet, muddy ground splashed around him. The itch and stink of the mud against his skin left him wallowing in discomfort. The tombstone rocked back and forth. Pastor Bernard screamed for forgiveness, but his cries were lost to the impact of the tombstone as it fell forward crushing him beneath its weight.

"Aaagh." Pastor Bernard shot forward into a sitting position. His body was drenched with sweat and his heart raced so loudly that it woke his wife from her slumber.

"Bernard, are you having another one of those nightmares?" Silvia said while wiping the crust of sleep from her eyes.

"Go back to sleep, Silvia. I'm fine. It was just a dream."

"You sure you don't wanna talk about it, baby?" Silvia sighed.

"It's nothing. Really, just go back to sleep." Pastor Bernard pulled back the covers and stood from the sweaty bed.

"Bernard, the bed is soaking wet. A few more minutes of nothing and you would've drowned us both. You need to tell me what's on your mind, honey."

"We both know what's on my mind." The pastor shrugged with annoyance.

"God, Bernard. How many times are we going to have to go through this? It's been 8 years. You did the right thing. This town needs a pillar of righteousness. That's you. You're the man of God, and your image as the pastor must be protected above all else," Silvia pleaded.

"Above all else, huh? How many times can I look that little girl in her eyes and maintain this lie? I can't live like this. I can't." Pastor Bernard wept.

"Man up." Silvia leapt from the bed and slapped Pastor Bernard with the ferocity of a cheetah. "This is bigger than you. It's bigger than that little girl. Besides, she's happy. HoneyBea is taking great care of her, much better care than that tramp of a woman ever could have."

"That tramp of a woman is her mother," Pastor Bernard shouted in retaliation.

"And you are my husband, the single most important reverend in Hurley, Mississippi. These people look to you for God's word. You owe them and you owe the Lord God, Himself. Your life is no longer yours, Bernard. You belong to them. Man up and be the shepherd that you vowed to be." Silvia grabbed her bathrobe and slowly wrapped it around her body before exiting the room to leave Pastor Bernard alone with his demons.

Pastor Bernard dropped to his knees facing his bed and clasped his hands in preparation for prayer. He wanted his mind to be free of the imagery in his nightmares. The sight of the large tombstone repeatedly flashed his mind. Even though his hands were not really filled with mud, they were filthy with the stains of a mistake that he would never be able to take back.

As he struggled to calm his mind and focus on the prayer, the house phone disrupted all of his thoughts with its seemingly thunderous ring. He overheard his wife's distant voice as she answered it with a "hello."

There was a long, alarming pause and then torrents of light ushered into the bedroom as Silvia rushed through the door. "Bernard, get dressed now. We're going to the hospital. The Vazquez boy was just hit by a drunk driver. Louise is hysterical."

"Oh God, no." Pastor Bernard gasped before jumping to his feet to face Silvia.

"Rumor was with him." Silvia hesitantly uttered.

"Rumor? How is she?"

"She's fine . . ." Before Silvia could finish her words, Pastor Bernard rushed past her out into the hallway.

It had to have been around two in the morning when Pastor Bernard and First Lady Silvia arrived at the hospital. I remember lying in Aunt HoneyBea's lap somewhere in between a state of sleep and unrest. It was late but Aunt HoneyBea didn't want to leave Taylor's mother Louise at the hospital alone. A surgeon was flown in from New Orleans to perform an emergency operation on Taylor. Louise cried non-stop as we waited for word on Taylor's condition. Aunt HoneyBea, who was usually full of appropriate words in difficult situations, had no idea how to calm Louise' sorrow, so she called the only person who would know. Pastor Bernard wore pajamas and a long blue bathrobe as he ran into the waiting room. I watched him as his eyes fixed on me. With the look that he gave me, you would've thought I was the one who had just been run down by a pick-up truck.

"Is she okay?" Pastor Bernard kneeled down and wiped hair out of my face as I lied stiffly on Aunt HoneyBea. I couldn't acknowledge him. I couldn't do anything but lie there fighting sleep while hoping to see Taylor's smiling face at any moment.

"Rumor's fine. She's just a little shook up. Louise needs you. We haven't heard anything from the doctors and that poor woman is losing her mind over there waiting," Aunt HoneyBea said.

"Oh, HoneyBea, we got here as soon as we could. Where is Taylor?" First Lady Silvia loudly stepped in with high heels and a cream colored pants suit. Somehow she managed to get dolled up at 2 a.m. in a time of crisis.

"I was just about to tell the pastor that he's in surgery. Louise needs you both. I mean her son is fighting for his life and her husband is on the run from the Hurley Police," Aunt HoneyBea explained.

"Oh my God. Manny? The police department? Why?" First Lady Silvia asked.

"Manny was drunk." Were the only words Aunt HoneyBea could muster; but by the looks on their faces, Pastor Bernard and Sister Silvia understood her perfectly. The swollen bags beneath Pastor Bernard's heavy eyes were the last sight I remembered seeing before falling asleep that night.

As I slept soundly against my auntie's warm body, Pastor Bernard struggled to calm his worries about my misery and focus on Louise. Louise Vazquez was a former beauty queen. Throughout her life, her face had always been her crowning glory. Naturally long, dark eyelashes surrounded the deepest and darkest eyes. When the sunlight hit her eyes from the perfect angle, an array of mocha brown shades were enough to capture the attention of anyone's stare. Her flawless, caramel colored skin contained a natural glow. At five feet, eleven inches tall, she stood high like a Mississippi Amazonian princess. Her rather thin physique held curves in all the right places, making her an immediate source of attraction for the men of Hurley.

Louise's father was the first man to fall victim to his daughter's enticing beauty. He felt that her beauty entitled her to treatment reserved for royalty. In order to satisfy his daughter's spoiled need for money and material things, Caesar Grimes dominated the cocaine industry. He became the number one source of the drug throughout Mississippi, Louisiana, and Alabama. The money was fast and Louise loved every second of it.

As a teenager, she was easily the most popular girl at Hurley High School. All the other girls envied her and all the guys wanted the pleasure of being her man, but Louise only wanted one man in particular. He was charismatic and full of life. His smile was enough to brighten any room. His personality alone was so addictive that Louise would not rest until he was hers. His friends called him Lucky. Lucky didn't possess amazingly good looks, athleticism, or style, but there was magnetism within his swagger that women could not resist. Lucky always got lucky.

Lucky was special to Louise. She'd easily gotten everything that she'd ever wanted in life, but he existed as her only challenge. Over the years, she coyly flirted, sending all kinds of signals his way. Lucky never took the bait. It puzzled her endlessly as to why Lucky did not pursue her like every other man in town. The more she thought about him, the deeper her infatuation with him grew. After years of desire, her pursuit of Lucky climaxed on the evening of the most important pageant of her career as a local beauty queen. It was the Sweet Tea of the Delta Debutante Beauty Pageant. Seven of the last ten women to represent Mississippi in the Miss America competition were former winners of the Sweet Tea of the Delta Beauty Pageant. Louise had her eyes on the competition for years, and everyone knew that she was a shoe-in as the winner. There was not one woman in the region who could challenge her beauty; and even if there was, her father had already bribed the judges with more money than most people could imagine.

Lucky's mother, Lula Mae, was the Mississippi director for the Sweet Tea of the Delta organization, and he sat attentively beside her with a smile that could eclipse the sun. Louise proudly strutted before the audience of Mississippi's elite like the true beauty queen that she was. She was on cloud nine as the crowd of spectators gazed upon her beauty, but what happened after she left the stage no one could have predicted. Another girl graced the stage. Louise stared at the girl with confusion. She didn't remember seeing her at any of the practices.

The girl was gorgeous. Everyone awed at the sight of her graceful beauty. She flowed across the stage like an angel in a white, satin floral gown with a silk bow around the waist. Louise cringed with envy as she watched Lucky's mouth drop at the sight of the angel soaring across the stage before him.

As the competition came to an end, the judges announced their choice. Louise's spirit shattered into painfully small fragments as the girl's name echoed throughout the auditorium. She could not believe what she was hearing. She did know the girl. The girl was a quiet, young freshman. The only time anyone would ever notice this girl was to pity her thick bifocals, her terrible case of acne, or the large metal braces that usually prevented her from keeping her mouth closed. This was not that girl. It couldn't have been her. Louise looked closely and slowly the resemblance became apparent. It was her. It was Alieza Arden. She was much younger, more graceful, and arguably more beautiful than Louise.

Louise was overcome with an emotion that she had never before felt in her then 17 years of life. She was ashamed. Although Alieza was much too young for Lucky's affection, Louise could feel that he desired her. Everyone did. Louise was no longer the center of Hurley's attention and her heart was broken. She wept for days. Her father, Caesar Grimes, was angered by his daughter's grief. He was determined that the city of Hurley would pay for humiliating his daughter. Caesar vowed revenge, but he started with the young man who had broken his daughter's heart. He started by ordering a hit on Lucky's life.

Caesar's goons beat Lucky within an inch of his life. The doctors had determined that there was no way Lucky would survive. His eternal wounds were too severe. Lula Mae did not accept that her son's fate was sealed. She sat by his side praying each day. She cried and begged for God to intervene. Months passed before God finally answered, but eventually Lucky opened his eyes from his coma. Caesar was arrested and sent to a state prison facility. Louise was left alone to suffer through poverty until she finally met and married a United States soldier by the name of Manny Vazquez.

Looking at her today, there were few signs of Louise's beauty queen past. Years of sorrow and abuse had left her less than a whisper of what she used to be. Pastor Bernard kneeled down before her and grabbed her shaking hands. He looked into her eyes as his mind searched for the correct words to speak. He couldn't say a word. Her pain was too overwhelming. He released her hand and slowly nudged upwards against her chin, raising her face into his view. She took one sight of him and her eyes immediately filled with tears.

"This wasn't supposed to be my life. My life was supposed to be with you. We would've been happy." Louise cried.

"Louise, I can't imagine . . ." Pastor Bernard struggled to speak as his own voice cracked with sadness.

"You wouldn't have hurt me like this. You aren't like Manny or my father. You wouldn't have abandoned me. You were supposed to be mine, Lucky." She dropped her head again before bursting into hysterical crying. Pastor Bernard held her in his arms as the weight of her grief consumed him. She reminded him of his own demons. She was a part of a past that he desperately needed to escape. He wanted to forget that he was ever known by the name, Lucky.

"Louise, God places us on certain paths for reasons that are unbeknownst to us, but we have to trust in his plan. Let's just pray for patience and guidance in the midst of this time of struggle." Pastor Bernard's voice shook with tension as he struggled to remain strong for Louise. His head was growing lighter by the second. As he clasped her hands into position for prayer, they both took alarm at the way he trembled.

"Honey, is everything okay?" First Lady Silvia approached from behind. By that time, the entire waiting room could feel the tension surmounting within the pastor.

Pastor Bernard did not answer her. He closed his eyes and proceeded to pray, but a bright light flashed within the darkness behind his closed lids. His eyes shot open with fright. He immediately fell backwards as the face before him was no longer Louise's. He slowly crawled backwards as creepy eyes surrounded by decaying flesh took sight of him. The sound of cracking bones and the smell of raw, rotten meat were heightened as the zombie woman stood to approach him. Fright consumed him. His muscles shut down leaving him immobile while facing the terror. The hospital lights shined brighter as the horrible figure stood in front of him.

"Get thee behind me Satan. My God said that the gates of hell shall not prevail against the church." Pastor Bernard's fear ridden voice erupted into a frantic yell.

"Gates that you opened, pastor. Don't speak to me of the church. The church stole my life from me. The church took me from my baby. The church has not begun to see hell, for hell hath no wrath like Alieza scorned." The rotting figure screamed.

"Alieza? Alieza, is that you? I'm sorry. I'm sorry. Oh my God, I'm sorry." Pastor Bernard wept.

"Bernard. Bernard, baby, it's me." First Lady Silvia attempted to quiet our frantic pastor, but it was too late. His mind was lost to guilt, and he'd already spoken my mother's name.

Something was torturing him and it was now clear that my mother was involved. I knew that I would never be able to count on anyone to be honest with me. The truth was out there. I just needed to figure out how exactly I would find it.

"Rumor, let's get you outta here, baby. You've got school in the morning. We'll come back to see Taylor tomorrow." Aunt HoneyBea quickly rushed me out of the hospital waiting room. She knew that I'd heard the pastor's frantic shouts to my mother. As she drove us both home, I could sense that there was something more that she wanted to say to me, but no words left her mouth.

By the time we pulled into the driveway of our home, rain, wind, and thick levels of fog had dominated the air. Veronya was still approaching, and like minions, her winds did not cease to taunt us. It was so dark that Aunt HoneyBea almost failed to see Darryl Junior as his car quickly swerved into the front yard as well.

"Boy. Have you lost your mind? I could've hit you. And where have you been anyway?" Aunt HoneyBea lowered the driver's side window to yell at Darryl Junior.

"My bad, Auntie, but we've got a serious problem on our hands." Darryl Junior lowered his window as well.

"I can't handle no more problems today. Rumor and I have had a long day. All I wanna do is go to sleep," Aunt HoneyBea said.

"Auntie, trust me when I say you're gonna want to handle this one."

"Boy, what is going on?" Aunt HoneyBea sighed.

"Well, we're gonna need to talk about this one alone," Darryl Junior explained.

"How's it going Ms. HoneyBea?" Chrisette's face came into view from the passenger seat as a flash of lightening illuminated the sky.

"Chrisette? Honey, is that you?" Aunt HoneyBea's eyes widened.

"Ay, is that my favorite Aunty?" Funyun's words slurred as he peered out from the back seat.

"Funyun and Chrisette? Boy this better be serious. Let me get Rumor to bed and I'll be back out." Aunt HoneyBea complained before continuing to park her car.

After an extremely long night combined with thunder, lightning and pouring rain; I couldn't help but fall asleep right away. Aunt HoneyBea sat beside our bedroom door and silently watched me as my heavy eyes eventually succumbed to slumber. I remember on that night, Taylor was the subject of my dreams. He smiled so wide that his small eyes seemed to be shut even as he looked at me. A scene of cumulus clouds and blue sky unfolded around us. Taylor reached out to grab my hands. Joyfully, I obliged. My mood was as cool as the sky around me. There was only Taylor and me accompanied by endless skies. With our hands connected, we danced in circles while jumping from cloud to cloud. A cool, comfortable breeze rushed around us as we navigated the heavens. I was so happy that I had not even noticed the small tear drop escape my right eye. I don't know if it was a tear of joy or of the sad realization that it was only a dream. Taylor stopped mid-step and released my hand. He scanned my face with concern before extending his hand to wipe the tear from my eye.

"Don't cry, Rumor. Joy comes in the morning." Taylor smiled while holding my tear drop in the palm of his hand. I looked down at the small drop of water and noticed an image forming within it. I looked closely and as the image became clear, I smiled at the sight of my mother's face. She was just as beautiful as the day that she left so many years before. I missed her.

"Alieza, what are you doing?" Aunt HoneyBea angrily stepped to my mother.

"I'm sorry, HoneyBea. I just wanted to see her. She's so beautiful." Alieza stood over me as I soundly slept dreaming of her presence.

"Do you know how long it took that girl to stop crying after you left here? Huh? Do you? You need to leave, Alieza. I don't know why Darryl Junior brought you back here, but I will have a long discussion with him about this later. As for now, you are not welcome in my home."

"But I'm your sister. Why are you always so mean to me?" Tears fell from Alieza's extremely thin and exhausted face.

"Mean to you? You haven't changed one bit. You meant the world to that child, and you abandoned her for 8 years. I refuse to let you hurt her again and I mean that baby sister."

"You know why I left and you know I had no choice. It's not like you had my back. You never did," Alieza retorted.

"Don't pull that 'woe is me' mess on me, Alieza. Everything that happened to you was your own fault. I warned you. I did everything I could to pull you from that path you were going down. You refused to listen to me. Do you think it was easy witnessing my baby sister lose herself? I had to wipe my hands clean of you for my own sanity. Now I would appreciate it if you catch the next bus back to Biloxi before you cause any more harm to that baby's life."

Alieza turned and gazed upon her sleeping daughter. It had been 8 years since she'd seen my face. Her baby had grown into a young woman and it hurt Alieza that she missed so many years. She couldn't erase any of the pain that she had caused. She couldn't help but think that maybe HoneyBea was right. Maybe the best thing for her daughter would be to continue on without her.

"Are you going to leave Alieza or am I going to have to put you out?" HoneyBea continued.

"Make sure my baby knows that her mama loves her, and you take care of her HoneyBea," Alieza cried.

"I always have," HoneyBea said while folding her arms across her chest.

"I'll stay with Champ until the storm passes. I'll catch the first bus back to Biloxi as soon as it does." Alieza reluctantly left but not before leaving a small envelope on the nightstand beside me. It was her weekly letter.

My Dearest Rumor,

I hope and pray that you know you are the reason I live and breathe each day. I look into the eyes of all these sweet children, and I see you. I see you every day. I can imagine that you're so tall by now. You're probably just as big as mommy. You probably have the clearest complexion of mocha brown skin. I'm sure it's smoother than the flat sands of the Sahara. I can imagine that your hair is long and full like the African lion. I can even imagine that sparkle in your eyes must be just as bright as the waters of the Nile River on a bright summer day. So much of Africa is beautiful, and although I know it is a blessing to be here improving upon the lives of these children, it is also a curse to be absent from the most beautiful part of me. That is you my Rumor.

Remember to look in the skies every morning. Stare right into the face of the Most High. Just as you are a reflection in his eyes so am I. And as long as we keep our eyes on Him, we'll always see one another. I miss you so much Rumor. Please always know that mommy loves you.

With deepest and sincerest love,

Your Mama, Alieza.

Rumor's Journal (Entry 4)

If she longs for me, then why say goodbye?
Her words I see, but why does she lie?
I miss her more than you could ever know,
Even though, of her, there is little that I know.
She is a mystery to me, a fool's lies in my head,
But somehow I still dream of her every night in my bed.
When will she return to usher in truth?
Vanquish the gossip and tales of uncouth.
I wait anxiously for her first step through my door,
Come back to me, I miss you, your Rumor

Chapter 5

Dawn of the Storm

The next morning I awoke to a sky which was almost as dark as the hole in my heart. The winds were beating against the windows as if they were demanding entrance. The lights within the house flickered off and on as the pressures of the weather grew to be too much for the electricity. The small light from well-lit candles illuminated a path into the hallway. Aunt HoneyBea's voice could be heard from the kitchen as she hummed the song, "This Little Light of Mine." Even with everything unfolding around me, the small white envelope marked "With Love, Alieza," still managed to capture my eyes. It was Tuesday morning and somehow the mail man was able to deliver her letter on time as usual. I wept as my eyes found each of her words. Her handwriting was not as neat as usual. It was clearly hers, but the writing seemed rushed. It was as if her emotions somehow bled through her words. The rough, scratchy look of each pen stroke varied like the erratic lines of a dying person's heart monitor. There was desperation in her handwriting. It was clear that this wasn't just any normal letter. As I continued to contemplate on the despair projecting from my mother's handwriting, an ominous feeling rose within me. I wasn't sure if this feeling came from the letter in my hands or from the loud stomping noise that grew closer to me with the passing of each second.

"Auntie, you seen my Mama's ring?" The floors shook beneath me as Gia stomped down the hallway while shouting questions to Aunt HoneyBea.

"Girl, ain't nobody wearing yo' mama's jewelry but you. Where you think you going anyway in this weather?" Aunt HoneyBea responded.

"It's just a lil' wind and rain. Plus I'm just going up the street to Princess' house. We gotta finish working on our group project for school." Gia undoubtedly lied. My cousin rarely did homework on school days, so I knew there was no way she was trying to do any on a storm day.

"Why you need your mama's ring for a school project?" By the sound of doubt in Aunt HoneyBea's tone, I could tell that she was not buying Gia's story either.

"I gotta have a reason to wear my mama's ring? Ugh. Ya'll get on my nerves. I can't wait to get out of this house," Gia fussed.

"Watch yo' mouth lil' girl. You'll be out there living in that hurricane," Aunt HoneyBea warned.

For a moment, Gia was quiet. She was a little too quiet. Aunt HoneyBea always said that the weather is most quiet before the storm. Without warning, our bedroom door flew wide open as Gia stepped inside to face me. Her right eye was raised slightly as the left one tightened into a scowl that expanded down to her lip which twisted to one side. Her arms were folded beneath her chest as she stood with her feet firmly planted beneath her. I could tell she was ready for war and unfortunately I was her chosen opponent. "This is your fault, Rumor. Ever since you went off on that lil' stupid hissy fit tearing up our room; my stuff has been missing."

"Gia, I haven't seen your ring." I boldly locked eyes with her angry expression. I was not about to let her scare me anymore. If it was a fight that she wanted, she had stepped to the right girl. Recent events had left me numb to all pain, so why would I fear her when I felt nothing?

"Don't get smart with me, Rumor. You think just because you had a lil' tantrum the other day and I didn't whoop your ass then that I won't whoop it right now?" Gia snapped.

"I'm not running," I replied with a steady, emotionless tone.

"Oh, well excuse me. It looks like somebody put on her big girl panties this morning, huh?" Gia stared harder into my eyes as if she was waiting for a sign of fear, but my expression did not change. I returned her stare with strong indifference.

"Okay then. Rumor wants to be a big girl. Well how about this for a big girl? You wanna sit your lil spoiled ass back and act out while everyone else babies you. Don't expect that from me, boo. I'm not the one. I'll tell you the truth." Gia flashed an unnerving smile. "How do you think that letter got here? Ain't no mail man running in this weather. Think about it. Alieza was here last night. Can't you smell the stink of fresh whore? It's still in the carpet."

"You're lying." I cried.

"Girl, please. You ain't important enough for me to be lying to. I'll leave that job to yo' mammy since she does such a good job of it anyway. She was here and she left your ass . . . again. You wanna know why? Because she hates you. Everybody hates you. Especially me." Gia continued.

"You know what, Gia? I hope you find your mama's ring," I said.

"Oh, really?" Gia asked.

"Really. I hope you find it in hell right after you give birth to that bastard you are hiding under your stomach right now. Oops. Was I not supposed to know that?" For the first time during our conversation, I smiled. It felt good to see the look of surprise on Gia's face. That moment was my first real taste of vengeance, and it was just as sweet as sugar.

"What the hell are you talking about?"

"We both know what I'm talking about, but I could be confused. Maybe I should go ask Aunt HoneyBea about that stick I found on your dresser when I had my temper tantrum," I said while mimicking innocence, which was now lost to me.

"Ugh. I hate you." Gia shouted before rushing out into the hallway.

As Gia disappeared into the candle lit hallway, I felt powerful. For the first time in a long time, I didn't feel like a helpless victim of life's circumstances. I felt like I was in control. I loved the feeling. I wanted more. I glanced down at my mother's letter and watched it crumble as I closed it into the palm of my fist. Then I walked out into the hallway, and lowered the balled up letter into the candle's fire. My eyes lit with satisfaction as the letter slowly burned into charred debris.

The small flame flickered before my eyes so beautifully. Glowing sparks created a trail of lights in the air around me. The sight of it all was so captivating that I almost didn't realize the flame was burning towards my hand. The growing heat of the flame slightly scorched my fingertips. I quickly released the burning paper and stomped out the flame before it grew to be uncontrollable.

"Lies." Before I could sweep away the burnt paper particles that now littered the floor beneath me, Aunt Mildred spoke from her corner in Aunt HoneyBea's bedroom. The slow creaking sound of her rocking chair as she swayed back and forth nearly gave me goose bumps. My first instinct was to disappear into my bedroom, but I could not look away from her.

"Lies." She repeated with a creepy tone. Her stare was locked on the toasted remnants of my mother's letter. I followed her gaze down to the burnt paper.

"Lies-a." She said again, but this time I heard her more clearly. For as long as I could remember, Aunt Mildred had always shouted lies when I came around. I always thought it was her way of taunting me; but for the first time, I understood. She was saying Lieza. Many people had told me that my resemblance to my mother during her teenage years was uncanny, but I always figured they were just being nice. My mother was so beautiful that I never really believed that I actually resembled her, but in that moment, I knew it was true. Because of Alzheimers, Aunt Mildred's mind was often stuck in the past. She wasn't talking to me. She was talking to someone who she thought to be her baby sister, Alieza Arden.

"Lieza? Was she here?" I replied while slowly approaching my aunt.

"Lies-a." She continued to chant as I excitedly fell into her arms. She held me tightly and smiled. "I missed you, Lies-a."

I cried. My tears poured onto her robe. I felt her embrace that was meant for my mother, and it was warmer than I could have ever imagined. The contempt growing within my heart suddenly stopped. I felt the love of my mother in my Aunt's arms. It made me miss her even more. Alieza Arden was somewhere in the city of Hurley; and while lying against Aunt Mildred, I knew that I would have to find her.

Below the creaking floor boards beneath Aunt Mildred's rocking chair, Chrisette had spent the previous night shivering in Darryl Junior's bed. As the winds of the approaching storm raged through Hurley, the temperature of the heatless basement grew more unbearable by the second. Chrisette attempted to clear her mind of the horrible weather long enough to fall asleep, but no amount of meditation could wipe out the loud roar of the storm's wind. After years of sleeping in the basement, Darryl Junior had grown accustomed to the unpredictable temperature; but Funyun's snoring was another story. Darryl Junior and Funyun were both lying in sleeping bags on the hard basement floor at the foot of the bed. With both his hands pressed tightly against his ears, Darryl Junior prayed for Funyun's snoring to cease. As if Funyun could hear his prayers, he replied with loud grunts and snorts before rolling over to blow the sound of his snoring directly into Darryl Junior's ear. Darryl Junior's nerves were on edge and he refused to listen to another second of Funyun's horrific snoring. He stood from the confines of his sleeping bag to see Chrisette both balled up and shivering beneath the sheets of his bed.

Her beautiful face was clinched tightly as she battled the cold from within her sleep. Darryl Junior lightly wiped his hand against her cheek. The brief sensation of his body heat sent a temporary look of peace across her face. The lines in her forehead cleared. Her flared nostrils deflated and her tightened lips fell to ease.

She was even more beautiful in comfort. Her brown skin was as smooth and moist as a pool of pure honey. Darryl Junior's heart longed for Chrisette. As much as he wanted to deny it, she was the only girl he had ever truly loved. The southern gentlemen within him did not want to disrespect her by climbing into the bed, but her sleeping body gave every signal that she longed for the heat that his body provided.

He pulled back the sheets and lied down behind her. Her tense arms were wrapped around her knees as she searched for comfort in the fetal position. Darryl Junior's strong arms were like the jaws of life as they seemed to yank her free of the cold. Chills flowed throughout her body as she was slowly overcome with warmth. His cologne lingered with a hint of familiarity in her nose. She was reminded of emotions that she'd thought were long gone. Darryl Junior could reach her heart like no other man could. Her instincts told her to push him away, but her skin craved his touch. She pushed her body backwards and closer to his. Darryl Junior smiled as her long, dark, silky hair flowed over his face. Her closeness was permission to embrace. He hugged her even more tightly as they both fell asleep under the comfort of the other's love.

"My man, Spade. That's what I'm talm bout. Get them drawers, dawg." The next morning, Funyun jumped to attention at the sight of Darryl Junior and Chrisette cuddled in bed together.

"What . . . wait . . . what happened?" Darryl slowly woke to wipe the crust of a good night's sleep from his eyes.

"Oh my God, get a life Funyun. Nothing happened. Tell him, Darryl." Chrisette rolled her eyes with irritation.

"Chrissy, quit frontin. I know my man, DJ the Spade, ain't spent a whole night on some tail without smashing." Funyun stretched out his hand to slap hands with Darryl Junior.

"Well, you know man, a gentlemen doesn't kiss and tell." Darryl Junior laughed and slapped hands with Funyun.

"You have got to be kidding me." Chrisette yelled at Darryl Junior.

"C'mon Chrissy. It's just Funyun being Funyun. You can't pay this man any attention," Darryl Junior said.

"Funyun's not a problem. It's you, you asshole. Get out of the bed." Chrisette screamed.

"Hold on baby. Chill. It's my bed." Darryl Junior pleaded.

"I said get out now." Chrisette screamed again before kicking Darryl Junior onto the floor.

"Forget her man. It's like you said, she nags too much anyway. You're the Spade, you can do better." Funyun retorted.

"I nag too much? Is that what you're telling people? You're pathetic, Darryl. And to think I rode out here to help you. You disgust me. I can't wait until this storm passes. Once we get back to Biloxi, I don't want to ever see your lying face again," Chrisette said.

Before Darryl Junior could respond, he was distracted by a loud knock from upstairs at the front door. "Darryl Junior." Aunt HoneyBea shouted his name shortly after answering the door.

"Chrisette, it's not like that. We'll talk about this after I see who's at the door, okay." Darryl Junior attempted to explain.

"I'm done talking. You're dismissed." Chrisette snapped. The sincerity within her tone was clear. Darryl Junior felt terrible, but he couldn't think of one word to console her over the sound of Aunt HoneyBea's yells from upstairs.

"What do you mean . . . evacuate? I've got food on the stove, and it'll be another hour before those ham hocks are finished cooking." Aunt HoneyBea stood before the light of the front door. As Darryl Junior approached, he could see Deputy Ron Mack on the other side of the screen door.

"I'm sorry Ms. HoneyBea, but the National Guard has warned the mayor that this storm is gonna be a hell of a lot worse than we thought. Mayor Clarke has ordered everybody to evacuate to the church dining hall. It'll be a lot safer there." Deputy Mack said.

"Young man, I have been living in this house for over 30 years. I have been through a lot worse than some wind and rain. Now if you'll excuse me, I've gotta go check on my ham hocks." Aunt HoneyBea pushed the door shut.

"Auntie, what are you doing?" Darryl Junior ran to catch the door. "Sorry 'bout that deputy. How long do we have before we should evacuate?"

"If you're asking for my suggestion, start packing now. Veronya's put a hurting on poor Cuba. If what we're about to get is anything close to what them Cubans got, things are about to get very ugly." Deputy Mack explained.

"Thanks Deputy Ron. We'll be heading to the church soon," Darryl Junior said.

"No, we won't either," Aunt HoneyBea stubbornly refuted.

"I'll work on her. Thanks again, deputy," Darryl Junior sighed.

"Is this storm over yet? I've got work to get back too." Chrisette angrily stomped out of the basement.

"Girl, you ain't goin nowhere on an empty stomach. Come on over here and help me with these ham hocks. You need to learn how to cook if you gon' keep my nephew happy. Boy eats like he got a tapeworm." Aunt HoneyBea smiled as if the wind were not beating our home like a drum.

"Ms. HoneyBea, I'll be glad to help, but with all due respect, your grandson's happiness is not my concern," Chrisette retorted.

"Not your concern? Boy, what did you do to this girl?" Aunt HoneyBea exclaimed.

"Auntie, you're going to have to pack those ham hocks to go. We're evacuating," Darryl Junior said.

"If you wanna evacuate, then honey don't let me stop you. I'm not leaving my house, boy," Aunt HoneyBea said.

"Evacuate? What's going on?" Chrisette asked.

"I smell ham hocks. When we eating?" Funyun stepped out of the basement to join them.

"We ain't eating nothing. We're going to the church where we were ordered to evacuate," Darryl Junior interjected.

"Gia, get in here and set this table, girl. Pull out the fine china. We got company." Aunt HoneyBea yelled while completely ignoring Darryl Junior.

"Auntie, listen to me. We can't stay here." Darryl Junior pleaded.

"Gia, don't you hear me calling you girl?" Aunt HoneyBea continued to yell.

"She's gone." Chrisette gasped. "Gia's gone."

"What?" Aunt HoneyBea shouted. "Rumor, where is Gia?"

"So is Rumor." Chrisette said.

"We're in the middle of a storm and you people just refuse to act right. What is this . . . the twilight zone?" Darryl Junior fumed with frustration.

"Sooo, we eating or not?" Funyun asked.

"Boy, shut up," Chrisette snapped.

"Darryl Junior, call Champ and see if they're over there. Lawd, please let them children be okay, cause I'm gonna kill 'em when I find 'em." Aunt HoneyBea cried.

As a storm of confusion broke out within the house, I sat outside determined to find my mother. Deputy Ron Mack's police car shifted under the pressures of the storm. His leather seats, wet with rain, squeaked beneath my movements. I watched as Ron ran towards the driver's side door and entered the car.

"Rumor, how'd you get out here?" Deputy Ron Mack took in the sight of me as I calmly sat on his passenger side seat.

"I'm going with you, deputy. My mom's in town and I need you to help me find her."

"If your mom is back in town, I'm sure your aunt will be happy to take you to her," Deputy Ron Mack said.

"No. She'll just lie about it. That's all they've ever done. You don't understand what it's like growing up without your mother. I need your help. I mean you are a policeman. Isn't that what you guys do? Protect and serve people?"

"Rumor, it's storming out here. Your aunt would be worried sick if you left."

"I'm with the police. I'll be safe," I responded.

"No, you're going to be with your family. C'mon. Get out of this car."

"Fine, but if you force me to go back in there, I'll be forced to tell my auntie that you and my underage cousin, who also just happens to be your little brother's girlfriend, are pregnant." I gazed into his eyes with the most convincing stare. I didn't know who the baby's father was, but based on the flirty eyes Ron Mack and

Gia exchanged Sunday morning, I was sure that he was a likely contender.

"Pregnant? What are you talking about?"

"She didn't tell you? Gia's pregnant. In fact, she's out somewhere in this storm as we speak with her friend, Princess. I'm sure Aunt HoneyBea is going crazy looking for her. Maybe I should shed some light on the whole situation." I slyly threatened while watching his eyes for some sign that my words were working.

"Rumor, I . . . I . . . I don't know what to say." As he spoke those words, I knew that my plan had worked.

"We've got a sighting of suspect Manny Vazquez in Mercy Projects on the intersection of Texas Street and MLK Drive. Suspect has been described as armed and dangerous. All available units requested for back up." Static interrupted our conversation before a man's voice sounded from Deputy Ron's radio.

"Crank it up, deputy. It looks like we've got a long day ahead of us." I smiled while buckling my seat belt and settling in for the ride.

"What in the hell have I gotten myself into?" Deputy Ron Mack shook his head from side to side before cranking the car for the drive towards Mercy Projects.

Rumor Journal Entry 5

When the winds sang,
They sang a song of everlasting rain.
A rain that drained the joy from our souls,
We were all left searching, both young and old.
There are answers in the storm so we must endure it,
A quest through chaos and we must pursue it.
Gloom today but prayers for joy in the morning,
No love lost, no message or warning.

Chapter 6

Lord Have Mercy

Of all the downtrodden areas in Hurley, Mercy Projects was by far the worst. Miles of red brick buildings covered unkempt grassy grounds and several corners of graffiti, prostitutes and drug dealers. The air was thick with clouds of pollution permeating from the large paper plant, Nelson Paper Manufacturers, which loomed a giant shadow over the largely neglected housing project. Even with a hurricane headed towards the city, the streets were filled with lost souls searching for survival. Manny Vazquez blended well among the area of misfits. With a 40 ounce bottle of liquor and a loaded glock 40 caliber pistol, Manny hid amongst the darkness of alleyways and bushes. The guilt of harming his only son had pushed his madness to a brink much further than that of his post-traumatic stress. He was an armed and intoxicated former soldier with no reason to live. Manny was a danger to anyone who breathed, and the streets were swarming with police cars searching for him.

Aside from the fact that red and blue police lights covered every corner of the city, the wind and rain had become unbearable with Veronya quickly approaching. Manny was forced to find some sort of shelter. With his face plastered over nearly every television screen, his quest proved to be a most difficult one. Deep in the heart of Mercy Projects, there was one apartment home that captured his attention. Beaded door curtains swung freely before the opened doorway of the quaint little apartment. He could only see candle light as he crouched low studying the apartment from across the street. A little old woman slowly walked by holding a black cat in her arms. As he listened to her conversing with the animal, it became clear that she was alone. Manny's drunken eyes locked tightly on his target.

The woman was a five foot tall Caribbean immigrant. She wore a bright, rainbow colored dashiki with a matching head wrap covering her head. She'd spent a lifetime studying the mythical arts of urban voodoo, and the smell of incense and exotic herbs traveling throughout her home gave a creepy vibe to the air surrounding her. Even with excessive amounts of alcohol pumping through his veins, Manny could feel his nerves trembling as he made his way into her home. A Caribbean drum beat combined with an exotic tune made up of flutes and rattle snakes played loudly from an old record player. Manny walked slowly with one hand on his gun, which was tucked away at his waist. The apartment was small, but the old woman did not appear to be anywhere in sight. It was as if she had vanished. Just as Manny loosened his grip on the gun, he was suddenly alarmed by the screeching of her cat as it pounced down upon him from the stairwell banister. Manny yanked the gun free of his pants and turned to face the old woman with a loaded barrel pointed in her direction.

"Calm down now, boy. Tuna no want problems." The old woman said while pushing the gun away from her face. She moved with indifference as if the man holding her at gunpoint posed no threat.

"Good, cause neither do I. I just need a place to stay for a while. You help me out and nobody gets hurt," Manny warned her.

"No refuge from life, young man. The dark spirits are all over you. I can feel them. You must face what you fear to save your soul."

"Chill with the crazy talk old lady. I just need to stay here for a lil' while. That's all. You can keep talking to your cat, and if anybody asks, you ain't seen me."

"Fine, young man. Me agree to help young brother. I am Maltooncha Ha' Awee, but most call me Tuna. You hungry? Tuna make fried guinea pig."

"Fried what? Nah. I'm good. I don't want no guinea pig. I'll just sit here on your sofa and mind my business until the storm passes, okay."

"More for Tuna." She laughed before disappearing behind another beaded doorway in the kitchen.

Manny felt as if he were sitting in some sort of time capsule from the 1970s. The floor was covered with lime green shag carpeting. The living room set was bright orange with green couch pillows. Small and large Caribbean tiki statues were placed on dressers and counter tops. African art covered the walls. There was no television or any sort of modern technology in the living room with the exception of an old record player.

Tuna's black cat cooed, purred, and rubbed its fur against Manny's leg. Manny hated animals, so he attempted to quietly shoo the cat away. The old woman's pet was persistent in her affections for Manny. She continued to cuddle beneath his leg. Manny became so annoyed with the cat that he kicked her causing her to shriek loudly.

"Sirene be a mischievous little one, don't she?" Tuna walked into the living room through the beaded doorway.

"Yeah, you might wanna get your cat before I put a bullet in her." Manny threatened.

"Steel fires no solve all of Manny's problems," Tuna chuckled with her thick Caribbean accent and broken English.

"How the hell do you know my name?" Manny quickly drew his gun and aimed for the old woman's cranium.

"The spirits tell Tuna that Manny coming," Tuna replied.

"You're lying. You talked to the cops, didn't you?" Manny jumped to his feet and quickly approached the woman.

"Tuna no have phone. Tuna only talk to spirits."

"Old woman, I swear I'll kill you. What did you tell them?" Manny yelled.

Before Tuna could respond, there was a knock at her front door. Manny's heart sunk within his chest. His fingers tightened around the gun's trigger. Within seconds, images of bombs exploding flashed throughout his mind. Soldiers yelled and screamed for cover as they dove within the trenches. Clouds of blood and sand flowed from around them. Manny quaked with terror as the worst of his military past resounded within his mind.

"Open the door, now." Manny stood waiting for his enemy to walk through the door.

On the other side of Tuna's front door, Gia was more nervous than she had ever been in her entire life. She tried to hide her nerves as Princess stared at her with condescending eyes, but there was no hiding the trembling of her hands. Her mind shifted back and forth over the repercussions of the decision she was about to make. She wanted to turn around and go home, but her legs would not move.

"Girl, stop being so scary. We goin' to Pensacola beach this summer and we wearing our bathing suit tops too. You can't be all out at the beach with no pregnant stomach. Unh Unh. That ain't cute boo boo," Princess argued.

"Ain't nobody scared. I'm just sayin'. How do you know that this woman knows what she is doing? This look like some backwoods mess to me. You got me all up in Mercy Projects. Girl, bye." Gia quickly retorted before turning to go back to Princess' car.

"Oh, hell naw. We done rode all the way out here. You gon' talk to this lady, Gia. Besides me and Miss Tuna go way back. Where you think I be getting my Dominican weaves from, girl? Tuna will hook you up."

"You want me to get an abortion from your weave lady? Are you serious?" Gia said.

"Gia, forreal, you need to quit trippin. How long we been friends, girl? I wouldn't ask you to do somethin' that ain't safe. My cousin's sister's best friend Rayniesha used Miss Tuna for like six abortions, girl."

"Six?"

"Hell yeah, girl. Six, and her uterus ain't never been scratched." Princess banged against the front door three more times.

"What's taking her so long, anyway? Dang, it is cold out here." Gia asked.

"Girl, I don't know. She prob out getting some eye of newt and toe of frog or some mess like that," Princess said before continuing to knock against the front door.

"Eye of newt?" Gia nervously replied just as the front door swung open.

"Tuna's been expecting you. Come on in." Tuna smiled as the two girls stepped through her doorway of beads.

When Deputy Ron Mack and I arrived at the place where Manny was spotted, swarms of police cars surrounded the apartment. It was like something out of an action movie as the deputies all stood around the front yard. Spectators stood against cars, trees, and anything else to battle the push of Veronya's powerful winds. They were all eager to see the action unfold.

"Stay low and don't make a sound, okay. Nobody can know you're here." Deputy Ron instructed before struggling to push the driver's door open. I could feel the slight shake of the car as the winds battled against it from the outside. The sky was as dark as midnight. The rain slowed to a slight drizzle, but occasional flashes of lightening served as warnings for the approaching storm.

"Just call me invisible." I spoke as the crashing of thunder nearly drowned out my voice completely. I wanted to watch for Manny's potential standoff with the police, but I couldn't risk being seen. The memory of seeing Taylor hurt and broken after being hit by the truck suddenly plagued me. How could a father run while his only son fought for his life? In that moment, I thought Manny had to be the lowest of human beings. I couldn't wait for him to get what he deserved.

As I stooped low in the backseat of the police cruiser, a loud piercing sound blasted across the sky. The sound rung throughout the city limits of Hurley. The high-pitched ring sent cold chills up my body. I sat nervously watching the sky through the rear window of the police car. The clouds appeared to merge instantly before my eyes. The massive clouds descended from the sky and swirled forming a frightening tornado. My eyes widened. My nerves trembled with fear. The large twister tore across Mercy projects while quickly heading towards us. A deafening scream filled the car. I pressed my hands firmly against my ears before I finally realized that the scream belonged to me.

Far on the other side of the city, hundreds of people sat stuffed inside the church dining hall waiting for Veronya. With the city's alarm ringing non-stop for the past five minutes, they knew that the storm could not be far away. Even the babies felt the pressure of the moment as they cried non-stop for what felt like hours. Mayor Thomas Clarke tried to keep the city's citizens calm, but people were growing more restless by the second. They had questions and they wanted answers. They needed to know how long this storm would last. How long their lives would be disrupted by this force of nature? The rumblings within the dining hall were growing to be too much for Mayor Clarke to handle.

"Sheila, where is Pastor Bernard? Doesn't he know he is making me look bad right before an election year?" Mayor Clarke stammered to his deputy mayor, Sheila Owen.

"The deacons are working on it, sir; but for now, you have to tell the people something. Come on, Mr. Mayor. I know you can handle it." Sheila tried to reassure the mayor, but even she doubted his ability to handle the situation. Mayor Clarke was a man of great fortune, but his social skills were seriously lacking.

"Tell them what? That this storm has gone from a category three to a five in only a matter of hours. That it will be the worst storm Hurley has seen in over 20 years. I can't do this, Sheila." Mayor Clarke continued to panic.

"Sir, just assure them that everything will be okay. Let them know that the city is taking every precaution to ensure the safety of them and their property. Like I said, I know you can do it, sir." Sheila forced an insincere smile for motivation.

"You're right, Sheila. Dammit, I'm a Clarke man. I've got this." Mayor Clarke shook off his nerves and stood with his head tall. He turned to face the dining hall full of people. Their anxious eyes were locked onto his every movement. They would be able to feel his fear, so he breathed deeply before approaching the podium. He stood there for a few seconds, taking in the sight of them all. They needed a savior. This was his perfect opportunity to earn their votes for re-election. At a time where Hurley's economy was at an all-time low, this would be his best chance of improving his forever sinking approval rating.

"The microphone is ready, sir. I'm right here behind you. You can do this." Sheila whispered so low that only Mayor Clarke could hear her.

"Aww hell, we're all going to die." Mayor Clarke burst into alarm before dropping his head to sob onto the podium.

"Well I'll be damned." Sheila flung her hands with frustration.

Outside of the dining hall, the deacons could hear the uproar of panic stemming from the town's citizens. They stood helplessly on the other side of a locked door begging Pastor Bernard to grant them entrance. Just as they were preparing to give up hope, the office door slowly swung open. They were not ready for what they saw on the other side.

Pastor Bernard sat shivering in the fetal position. His eyes were rounded and motionless. Communion wine dripped from over his head, down his clothes and onto the floor surrounding him. As they approached him, he did not move an inch. Deacon Hamilton knelt down facing him. He searched the pastor's catatonic eyes for some sign of the man that they had all depended on.

"Pastor, you've gotta come out here and help us. The whole town is in an uproar over this storm. We don't know what to do." Deacon Hamilton said.

"The life of flesh is in the blood, given to us to make atonement for our souls. It is the blood that makes atonement for the soul. Forgive us Lord. Cleanse us with the blood." Pastor Bernard erratically whispered bible scriptures.

"Please, reverend, we need you." Deacon Booker begged.

"Without the shedding of blood, there is no remission for sins." Pastor Bernard whispered again; but this time, he moved. He reached over his head and grabbed an opened bottle of wine from his desk. Before the deacons could stop him, he proceeded to pour the bottle of wine all over himself.

"What's wrong with him?" Deacon Booker asked as Deacon Hamilton wrestled the bottle of wine from the pastor's trembling hands.

"I don't know, but go get First Lady Silvia. I don't know what else to do." Deacon Hamilton commanded. Deacon Booker rushed out into the dining hall, scrambling through the crowds of panicking citizens searching for First Lady Silvia.

The First Lady, ignorant to her husband's mental state, sashayed through the dining hall attempting to calm as many people as possible. She took notice of Aunt HoneyBea in the corner using the church's phone. Whatever Aunt HoneyBea was talking about, she seemed to be frustrated. First Lady Silvia's curiosity peeked as she stepped closer to eavesdrop on the conversation.

"Champ, I can't take all of this. It's bad enough that Rumor and Gia are out there somewhere in that storm. I don't need you out there in that mess too. Sheriff Mack and his deputies are looking for the girls. You and Alieza need to get somewhere safe. They say this storm is gonna be bad," Aunt HoneyBea said.

"Sis, I can't let Alieza go out there alone, and she is determined to find Rumor. Plus we heard that the sheriff and all the deputies are held up in Mercy Projects on a standoff with Manny Vazquez." Uncle Champ explained.

"What? They found Manny. Jesus, I hope Rumor isn't somehow mixed up in this mess. That girl ain't been the same since Manny hit Taylor with that truck." Aunt HoneyBea sighed deeply while pondering about Rumor's whereabouts.

"You think Rumor may be in Mercy?" Uncle Champ asked.

"I don't know Champ, but nobody's seen her since Deputy Ron left the house earlier. I wouldn't be . . ." Before Aunt HoneyBea could finish speaking on her thoughts, Alieza mashed the horn of Uncle Champ's car several times making it clear that she was ready to go.

"Sorry HoneyBea, but you know your sister. Let me get out here before that girl drives off in my car."

"Tell that chile to hold her horses!" Aunt HoneyBea exclaimed.

"Oh shoot, gotta go. She's moving," Uncle Champ yelled before hanging up the phone and making a dash for the car.

Aunt HoneyBea stared nervously at the phone's receiver for a few seconds before finally hanging up. Her heart was heavy for the current state of her family. She couldn't help but blame herself. Ever since their mother died, Aunt HoneyBea had always been the glue that held the family together. Her first mistake was allowing Alieza to leave. Even after all of the harm that her baby sister had caused, Aunt HoneyBea knew that their mother would not have been happy with that decision. Then she couldn't help but contemplate on my situation. No child should have to grow up without her mother. If for no other reason, she knew that she should have protected Alieza for me.

"Beatrice, hun, are you crying?" Sister Emmagene appeared pulling a pink handkerchief from her purse.

"No, I'm fine. I just got something in my eye," Aunt HoneyBea lied.

"Beatrice, girl, you don't have to lie to me. Tell me what's going on. I'm here for you, honey. I mean what are friends for, anyway?" Sister Emmagene persisted.

"It's HoneyBea. Oh, nevermind. I need to go find my nephew," Aunt HoneyBea said trying her best to elude Sister Emmagene's prying questions.

"He and that pretty young lady went to the storage closet to set up the generator in case the lights go out. They may be a while." Sister Emmagene smiled knowing that she had thwarted my Aunt's means of avoiding her.

"Oh. He and Chrisette. They must've left Funyun behind?" Aunt HoneyBea asked.

"You talking about that crude, awful young man? Why is it that your children entertain such animals? You definitely have my sympathies, hunny. Between Gia courting with that rapping fool and Darryl Junior traveling with that farting freak show, I don't know how you do it." Sister Emmagene returned to her normal condescending tone.

"Well, something tells me you'll be figuring that out very soon, Sister Emmagene." Aunt HoneyBea smiled.

"Why do you say that?" Sister Emmagene asked.

"Well, it looks like Funyun's getting awfully familiar with your oldest daughter right now. Poor girl seems to be having a good time too." Aunt HoneyBea chuckled while taking sight of Funyun as he flirted with Sister Emmagene's daughter, Nivea.

"Huh? Nivea," Sister Emmagene squealed before turning to fetch her daughter from Funyun's grasp. Aunt HoneyBea released a breath of relief before continuing to silently reflect on her family.

Sister Silvia, who was still silently eavesdropping on my Aunt, stepped into view to grab the phone for herself. "HoneyBea, how is everything?" First Lady Silvia asked.

"I'm fine, First Lady. I was just about to go find my nephew in this crowd," Aunt Honey Bea answered.

"Great. You mind if I make a call real quick. It's kinda' personal." First Lady Silvia flashed an insincere smile as Aunt HoneyBea walked away.

In the church's storage closet, Darryl Junior and Chrisette both stood within the tight, dusty space searching for the generator. With flashlights as their only light, they quickly rummaged through each shelf. They hadn't spoken one word to one another since leaving the dining hall. Chrisette glanced backwards over her right shoulder as Darryl Junior sneezed from the clouds of dust permeating from one shelf.

"God bless you," she said.

"You're talking to me now?" Darryl Junior asked.

"Look, Darryl, I'm sorry for blowing up on you earlier. You're not my man and I've gotta stop placing these expectations on you. Besides, we're here for your family. You don't need me adding extra stress to the situation," Chrisette apologized.

"But see that's just the thing, Chrisette, I want you to be a part of my family. That's why I asked you to come," Darryl Junior confessed.

"That's sweet, Darryl, but we've tried this before. It just doesn't seem to work for us."

"C'mon, Chrissy. You came all the way out to Hurley just because I asked you to. I know you don't just go around taking road trips at the drop of a dime for just any old cat. We obviously still care about each other. Why not give it another try?"

"Honestly, when I saw the way you rescued your aunt back at the casino, I saw a look in your eye. It was a look that I hadn't seen in a long time. I saw Darryl Junior. Not DJ the Spade. I guess I just hoped that by coming back to Hurley with you I would see more of Darryl. I miss him." The light of Darryl Junior's flashlight highlighted a tear dropping from Chrisette's eye as she spoke.

"I'm always Darryl Junior, Chrissy. I just have to handle business differently when I'm running my company. I don't get how you, of all people, don't understand that."

"I understand DJ when it comes to business, but what I'll never understand is why you have to be DJ when it comes to me," Chrisette cried.

"I know that I hurt you when we were together, but you've gotta believe that I didn't mean those things that I said to you the night that we broke up. I was stupid and . . ." Darryl Junior hesitated to finish his statement while recalling the night that he and Chrisette ended their relationship. In his mind, he could see Chrisette's teary eyes as he smiled and primped in the midst of clients. He was entertaining a few A-list rappers to book them for a summer concert. What better way to entertain rappers than with gorgeous groupies. Amongst Darryl Junior's selected groupies, stood Olivia Wright, the most desired woman in Mississippi. Darryl hoped that Olivia's seductive ways would help to seal the deal with the entertainers, but he soon discovered that he had bitten off more than he could chew with Olivia Wright. Olivia was not interested in any ignorant rappers. She was intrigued by Darryl Junior's business savvy and swagger. It wasn't long before her roaming hands found the most private parts of Darryl Junior's body. Darryl tried to contain Olivia's roaming hands, but he knew that he was too late when he saw Chrisette stomping towards them. He wanted to explain everything to Chrisette. He wanted to kiss her passionately and remind her that she was the only woman for him. He never wanted to lose her but his ambitions would not allow him to risk losing the deal. He knew that he would lose the respect of the rappers if he seemed to be weak in front of his woman. Chrisette stormed out of the casino in tears as Darryl Junior remained in the company of rappers and groupies struggling to maintain the reputation of DJ the Spade.

"And what? Go ahead, say it Darryl. You had to be the Spade in front of your clients. The Spade wouldn't dare love a woman over his money. I'll always come second to the Spade. That's not a life that I'm willing to live," Chrisette angrily replied while wiping the tears from her eyes.

"You won't have to. I promise. You said yourself that you saw a different side of me before we left the casino. I'm willing and ready to give this all up for the people that I love and that includes you. Chrissy, I gave away all my shares of Gulf Gamble stock. I don't have any more control in Biloxi. I'm ready to be Darryl Junior again." Darryl Junior reached out and wiped a tear from Chrisette's eye.

His Gulf Gamble stock was the key to his influence over the Biloxi nightlife. Gulf Gamble was the one corporation which held majority stock in most of Biloxi's casinos. Most of the casino owners sought startup capital from the corporation to fund their casinos in exchange for ownership. Darryl Junior, being the expert business man that he had become, used the majority of his casino winnings and promotion earnings to buy stock in Gulf Gamble. It was his ownership in Gulf Gamble that helped him solidify himself as the promotion king of Biloxi.

"Really? Why would you do that?" Chrisette shot Darryl Junior a look of confusion.

"For us. I've made my money, Chrissy. I've been thinking about this for a while now. I'm gonna let Red run D Spade Promotions for a while. I'm gonna focus on becoming a man for my family and for you if you'll have me." Darryl Junior pulled Chrisette into a tight embrace.

"You don't know how long I've waited to hear you say those words. I love you, Darryl." Chrisette returned Darryl Junior's hug while weeping on his shoulder.

"I love you too, Chrissy," Darryl Junior replied.

"Wow. I can't believe you gave away your stock. Who'd you give it to, anyway?" Chrisette asked.

"Caesar Grimes. He gave Alieza freedom in exchange for the stock."

"Caesar? You gave your Gulf Gamble stock to Caesar Grimes?" Chrisette pushed herself free of Darryl Junior's embrace.

"Yea. What's the problem?"

"Darryl, are you serious? Caesar Grimes has been trying to get stock in Gulf Gamble ever since he was released from prison. He's going to take control of the casinos, my father's included."

"Chrissy, what are you talking about?"

"Caesar Grimes has been threatening casino owners for months now in exchange for a percentage of their earnings. He tried to do the same to my father last month, but my old man turned him in to the Biloxi PD. Caesar's been threatening us ever since by saying that he's going to take my father's casino, and you just gave him what he needs to do it."

"Chrissy, I didn't know," Darryl Junior pleaded.

"I should've known. You are like poison to me," Chrisette said backing away from Darryl Junior.

"Chrissy, you can't be serious," Darryl Junior said reaching for her.

"Just stay away from me." As Chrisette screamed, the winds gained force from outside.

The hallway lights flickered bringing a greater degree of darkness to the storage closet. A loud crashing noise sounded as a tree up-rooted and fell onto the church. The building trembled. The storage closet door slammed shut. Shelves began to fall all around them as clouds of dust made their air nearly impossible to breathe.

Meanwhile, the dining hall continued to shake beneath the impact of the tree. The already panicking citizens were even further stirred by fright. Chaos erupted within the dining hall until everyone's attention was captured by an even greater chaos unfolding in the center of the floor.

Pastor Bernard stood nude in the middle of the floor covered with red wine. The wine flowed down over his face and body like blood. "Repent. The time of judgment is upon us. Repent. The Lord has unleashed his wrath. We will all pay for the sins of this city. Repent . . ."

First Lady Silvia's face was frozen with shock as the phone receiver hung loosely from her ear. She nearly dropped the phone until the deep hoarse voice on the other end revived her. "Silvia, you still there?"

First Lady Silvia tightened her grip on the phone receiver and pushed it closer to her ear, "He's losing his mind, Caesar. I don't know how much longer I can do this."

"Calm down, Silvia. Everything is going according to plan. Trust me; you won't have to deal with the soon to be departed reverend for much longer," Caesar assured her.

"Trust you? I overheard HoneyBea on the phone earlier. Alieza has returned. How could you allow that?" the first lady protested.

"Alieza is my final pawn. I now have a majority ownership of Gulf Gamble, so be patient my love. Caesar Grimes is back on top. The city of Hurley will soon know the full extent of my vengeance." Caesar's confidence could be heard clearly within the tone of his voice.

"That sounds like music to my ears, Baby. Hurry. I can't wait to plant a kiss on those wealthy lips." First Lady Silvia giggled before hanging up the phone.

Fully distracted by the powerful storm that raged its way across the city, the people of Hurley had no idea that their greatest challenge was just across the horizon. Caesar Grimes pulled against the lapels of his suit jacket ensuring that he looked his best for the confrontation that awaited him in Hurley. Caesar felt wronged by the city that turned its back on him. After spending years in prison, he had more than enough time to contemplate on his revenge. Now that his plan was in action, there was no containing the pride that swelled within him.

Caesar's former lady of the night, Alieza, sped down the streets of Hurley searching frantically for me, her only daughter. Uncle Champ sat in the passenger seat pleading for my mother to slow down as she carelessly navigated the streets. He almost regretted telling her about Aunt HoneyBea's thoughts on the possibility of me being in Mercy Projects with Deputy Ron. The disc jockey speaking from the car stereo warned of the terrible tornado that swept through Mercy Projects. Uncle Champ wanted to wait until the weather calmed, but he knew by the intense stare of determination in Alieza's eyes that there was no way she would turn back.

While still crouching low in the back of the police cruiser, my loud screams were lost to the blowing of Veronya's tornado which tore through Mercy Projects. The squad of deputies in Miss Tuna's front yard raced for their cars. Ron Mack ordered them to stand their ground, but his commands were outranked by the approaching whirlwind. Manny took full advantage of the moment and sprayed a round of bullets out into the front yard. Ron quickly ducked for cover. Manny's mind was still fixated on his days of war. He imagined that officers were among the enemy's ranks. Each shot was intended for an Iraqi soldier in the Cold War. Seeing that his enemies were frazzled by his initial round of fire, Manny grabbed Gia as a hostage and ran out into the front yard. Princess screamed for help but nothing but the howling of Veronya's winds could be heard.

A leaning power line swayed beneath the pressure of the winds. One of the poles holding the power lines in place cracked and fell onto a police cruiser below. The flailing power line traveled down to the ground with the broken pole. The damaged police cruiser leaked oil onto the ground, which ignited into a blaze upon contact with the loose power line. With Veronya's winds feeding the fire, the entire front yard filled with flames. Manny held Gia closely as he raced through the front yard careful to avoid the growing flames. Gia screamed and cried for help, but Manny held her at gun point, preventing her from getting away. Deputy Ron followed the path of Gia's screams while racing to her rescue. With the knowledge that she was possibly carrying his child, there was no way Ron was going to let Manny harm Gia. Ron leapt behind one of the police cruisers and took aim of Manny as he ran. With his gun in focus, Ron took the shot. Manny stumbled as a bullet traveled into his right thigh, but he did not release his grip on Gia. Manny quickly returned fire. Deputy Ron attempted to dive for cover, but not before Manny was able to hit him with a bullet to his shoulder. Ron fell to the ground, writhing in pain.

Manny located the only empty police cruiser and pushed Gia inside. He quickly followed. Luckily, the keys were still in the ignition. Before Ron could stand to his feet, Manny mashed the gas leaving only a trail of dust behind him. From the back of the police car, I could see Gia crying frantically. The terror in her eyes gave her a vulnerability that I'd never seen before from Gia. Manny yelled for her to shut up. He pointed the gun in her direction as he drove. Flashbacks of Taylor's twisted body, after being hit by Manny's truck, invaded my mind. I knew that I couldn't let Manny hurt Gia too, so I screamed. I screamed as loud as possible. Gia looked down and saw that it was me in the back of the car. Her eyes widened as Manny turned to send a round of gun fire in my direction.

"Rumor, noooo," Gia screamed while kicking Manny with all of her strength. Manny dropped the gun as one of Gia's kicks landed firmly against his arm. Infuriated, he grabbed her legs and pushed them both aside. Gia swung wildly with both of her arms to fight him off, but Manny was too strong for her. He punched aiming for her face, but as Gia shifted to avoid the blow, his punch landed against her stomach. The pain in Gia's stomach felt as if she had just been crushed by boulders. She grabbed her stomach tightly trying to contain the sting of the pain, but it couldn't be contained. It quickly shot throughout her body. Overcome with anguish, she kicked free of Manny's grip and knocked him unconscious with a swift knee to the head. Manny fell backwards as the car spun out of control.

The screeching of tires and the honking of a car horn caught us off guard as the police cruiser was struck by another approaching vehicle. I fell forward hitting my head against the back of the driver's seat. Through dazed and blurred eyes, I looked up to check on Gia. My head throbbed with pain. Blood was all over the shattered wind shield. Someone had been thrown from the car and she lied lifeless against our windshield. As my vision became focused, the bloody face lying on the windshield looked familiar. Her eyes were open but motionless. Those same eyes were the subject of many of my dreams over the years. I gasped at the sight of my mother staring at me through lifeless eyes. Blood drained from her head. I was speechless.

"Aaaagh . . . My baby," Gia screamed frantically. Pints of blood flowed freely from beneath her skirt. Her hands were covered with it. There was only one heart beat in her body, which only minutes before held two; and by the look on my cousin's face, it was clear that she would never be the same.

Rumor's Journal (Entry 6)

No words to say,
It is as if the winds came and blew them all away.
Can't think of a single thought worth being said,
Now that my reason for living is dead.
Cold eyes laid to sleep,
While dark images in my mind still burn deep.
To look into opened eyes but no one looks back,
Is a fright more severe than a thousand heart attacks.
Like flies and filth, true decay consumes her.
All she left behind was one bitter Rumor.

Chapter 7

The Crushed Berry Mural

I can still remember her smiling face. She looked beautiful as the sunlight cascaded down through her long, flowing hair. Her smile was broad, which caused her eyes to squint into tight little bulbs of happiness. She tickled me gently as my little body squirmed and laughed from within her arms.

"Who are you, Rumor?" I could hear my mother asking in my memories.

"My mama's baby," I giggled in return while she continued to tickle me.

"That's right. You'll always be mama's baby," she said before kissing me softly on my forehead.

I was only three years old at the time, but somehow that memory, which had long been lost to the earliest years of my youth, returned to me. She said that I would always be her baby. She had lied to me. Everyone lied. All that I knew were lies, and living a lie is like jumping into a pool of blades on a daily basis. You're constantly trying to swim through life without having to face the truth behind the lies that you've created. If you make one wrong move, you'll be cut with the pain of a thousand lies, each one multiplied over time just to hide one single truth. The result is almost always a pool of blood.

Over the past few days so much blood had been spilled. Pints of blood spread out over a cracked windshield, completely blinding me to the outside world. The only visible sight was her eyes. Her pupils were motionless as her stare seemed to lock upon me. It was as if she stared at me from the afterlife. I couldn't remove the sight from my mind. It reappeared constantly as the end of a stream of images constantly moving through my imagination. There was Taylor's blood-covered, broken body; the growing blood stains on Manny's thigh and Deputy Ron's shoulder; and Gia's womb as it birthed forth the remains of her bleeding child. Behind shut lids, my mind was being haunted by these sights; but before opened eyes, my arm still bled from the glass of Gia's shattered dresser mirror. My bandages had become completely red as I squeezed tightly against my wound. The pain that resulted from my arm was like a gift for that moment. The physical pain was the only relief I could find from my emotional scars.

"Rumor, what are you doing?" Sheriff Mack spotted me as I purposely disrupted my cuts. "Somebody get me some clean bandages over here."

He knelt down before me as one of his deputies approached with a roll of fresh bandages. There was a look of concern in his eyes as he scanned my bleeding arms. His touch was gentle as he carefully cleaned my cuts before applying the bandages. "Rumor, you've been through a lot. I can't imagine what you're feeling right now, but hurting yourself is not the answer baby girl." I said nothing in return. He had no idea the pain that I was feeling. No one did. The sight of my mother's death would forever plague my mind.

Veronya had passed and the weather was calm. I sat behind Sheriff Mack's desk in the midst of a crowded police station. The phones were ringing off the hooks. Deputies and other Sheriff Department employees rushed back and forth busily attending to the aftermath of the storm. Deputy Ron Mack and Gia were both rushed to the hospital hours before. Uncle Champ was in one of the interrogation rooms answering questions for the police report. As a minor who had just witnessed the death of her mother, the police decided to delay my questioning until a later time. Sheriff Mack tried his best to get my mind off the situation while my uncle was being questioned. He offered me snacks from the vending machines, but my taste buds were numb. He told me funny police stories, but I could not find a place for laughter within me. He attempted to counsel me, but

I had not spoken one word since they pried my shocked body from the back of the police cruiser. Low on options, Sheriff Mack tried his best to hide the worry that was clearly within him, from me.

"Well Sheriff, unless you guys have anything else you need from me, I think I'm gonna get my niece home." Uncle Champ approached the sheriff's desk. My uncle's tired eyes were surrounded with the lines of grief. His face seemed to sag beneath the weight of his frown. I'd never seen Uncle Champ so low on energy. With only one bandage wrapped around his forehead from the impact of the airbag, Uncle Champ was very fortunate in the car accident. He took one look at the amount of hurt on my face and nearly lost his composure. It took every piece of strength within him not to break down in front of me. He wished that it had been him who was thrown through the car's windshield. In his mind, he couldn't stop asking God why he had been spared when his baby sister lied cold and lifeless in a body bag.

"No. There's nothing else. Please get baby girl home to her family. You guys are in my prayers. Let me know if your family needs anything. The Mack's are here for you." Sheriff Mack tried his best to console my uncle.

"Thanks Sheriff. C'mon Rumor. Let me get you home."

As Uncle Champ escorted me out of the police station, the old Caribbean woman sat eyeing me from behind one of the deputy's desks. She looked at me as if she had seen me before. She mouthed the word, "Alieza." My eyes immediately widened. I snatched my hand free of Uncle Champ's grip and rushed to the desk to face the old woman. I didn't say a word. The curiosity in my eyes did all the speaking.

"She came to see Tuna many years ago. She looked like you, Chile. The same beautiful face, but a heart broken in two by life. The truth of her is near you. Closer than you think. Many hold two faces, but the truth you seek lies behind only one," Miss Tuna whispered.

"Stay away from my niece old woman. She's been through enough without you putting all that devilish cockamamie nonsense in her head," Uncle Champ retorted while pulling me away from Miss Tuna.

"Tuna mean no harm. Bye, chile." Miss Tuna flashed her creepy grin of tobacco-stained teeth. As bizarre as she appeared, there was still something very genuine about Miss Tuna. Somehow I knew that she was telling the truth. Miss Tuna may have been a very bizarre old woman, but unlike my Uncle, I believed everything she'd said. She had known my mother. Everyone knew her, and I lived as the only exception.

The next couple of days seemed to be one giant blur. Veronya had left the city of Hurley in ruins. People's homes and other forms of property were left devastated by the damages. Many areas suffered from flooding. Blackouts plagued the city as the local electrical company scrambled to attend to downed power lines. The number of injuries was countless, but the number of deaths was very few. On May 6, 2003, my mother Alieza Arden was one of only three deaths to occur in Hurley, Mississippi, during Hurricane Veronya. Gia's unborn and unnamed child was also among the three fatalities. The third death was confirmed to be local drug dealer, Tavis Tahiri. Tavis was the older brother of the Tahiri triplets. According to news reports, Tavis' cause of death was still unknown. His body was reportedly unrecognizable. Authorities had found his identification only inches away from the body. Police were investigating further to determine whether his death would be handled as a homicide. Just the thought of homicide was enough to thicken the air of gloom that had congested Hurley's air. Even with the crime-filled streets of Mercy Projects, homicides were very rare in Hurley. The city was on edge as the local news provided updates on the possible murder of one of its own.

"I've always been a strong advocate for burning that place down from day one. There are nothing but druggies and hoodlums over there in Mercy Projects. While we're wasting our tax payer dollars to support them, they're driving up the city's crime rate." Sister Emmagene stood with her hands planted on her hips. She was eyeing the television screen as if she could see through it. As she spoke, Aunt HoneyBea rummaged through the pantry causing pots and pans to sound off as she pushed them to the side. Even until this day, I believe that she was making those noises on purpose to drown out Sister Emmagene's constant complaining.

Sister Emmagene's home was among the houses destroyed by Hurricane Veronya. The leaders of the church implemented a program to ensure that those left homeless by the hurricane would be provided shelter until they could have their homes rebuilt. Sister Emmagene was not willing to have herself or her daughters cramped up in anyone's home except for that of the only woman she considered to be her friend, Aunt HoneyBea. Aunt HoneyBea cringed while agreeing to open her home to the woman she wanted so desperately to avoid.

"Beatrice, honey, there's static all over the television. Did you remember to pay your cable?" Sister Emmagene yelled without removing her eyes from the television screen.

"That's it. I'm about to find that cable and wrap it around her worrisome throat," Aunt HoneyBea said while slamming a frying pan against the stove.

"Now cousin HoneyBea, I'm gonna need you to calm down. You don't wanna get your pressure up again, do you?" Cousin Junebug said attempting to calm my aunt's temper. Cousin Junebug was only one of the many members of our family who traveled down to Hurley from Chicago for my mother's funeral. Between Sister Emmagene, her three daughters, and a few Chicago members of our family, Aunt HoneyBea's house was full of guests.

"My pressure? Junebug, my pressure went through the roof yesterday when Cousin Lonnie tried to burn Cousin Lay Lay with a candle at the funeral home. My pressure went through the roof when Great Cousin Jeb's see-and-eye dog pissed all over my new hardwood floor.

It even darn near exploded when Omar's bad-behind kids decided they were gonna roll Mildred outside to play hop-scotch in traffic. Now that woman in there, she is about to give me a full on stroke," Aunt HoneyBea fussed. Ever since my mother's death, Aunt HoneyBea purposely overwhelmed herself with planning every detail of the funeral. The preparations were exhausting, especially with her being responsible for bringing our outrageous family into one setting, but I think she appreciated the distraction from mourning.

It was Friday morning, more than 48 hours since I'd left the Sheriff's department; and I still had not spoken one word. I spent my days squeezing my injured arm, searching for every bit of pain that I could find to distract from that week's tragedies. Once I was satisfied with the damage that I'd inflicted upon myself, I treated and re-bandaged my own wounds. I didn't want Aunt HoneyBea to know what I was doing to myself. I didn't want anyone to know. I was ashamed of my state of mind, but there was nothing I could do about the sight of my mother's dead eyes which was permanently stained on my mind.

Gia hadn't said many words since the accident either. Her normally vibrant face was pale and dry. Gia would usually spend hours each morning in the bathroom attending to her looks but even that had changed. Her hair had been pulled back into that same pony tail for the past two days. She dawdled around the house in her pajamas, barely ate anything, and spent the majority of her time sleeping in bed. She was even starting to smell a little as she hadn't showered once since arriving home from the hospital.

She and I were both silent as Sister Emmagene's daughters: Nivea, Cora, and Ashley invaded our room. Nivea was the same age as Gia. They were in the same classes at school and Nivea worshipped the ground Gia walked on. As bad as Sister Emmagene wanted to be my aunt's friend, I believe Nivea wanted to be Gia's friend ten times more. She followed Gia around waiting on her hand and foot while serving her every need. Cora was around my age and she couldn't be any more different than Nivea. Cora was spoiled and conceited in every way possible. She complained about everything. She complained about our rooms, the paint color on our walls, the food we ate, the clothes we wore, and any other thing she could think of that didn't meet her little princess standards. Ashley, the youngest daughter, was only six years old, but she was a meddlesome terror. She broke everything that she put her hands on and there wasn't much that she didn't touch.

To avoid our overwhelming house guests, I spent most of my time with Aunt Mildred. Somehow I wasn't afraid of her anymore. In fact, we grew closer during my days of silence. I would lie on her lap as she rocked away on her rocking chair. Neither of us would speak, but somehow I felt she understood me more than anyone in the house.

Darryl Junior shared his space in the basement with Cousin Junebug. He hadn't been to work in Biloxi since the hurricane hit, but not because of any kind of mourning. Darryl Junior was suffering from a broken heart. After a tree fell onto the Church's dining hall, the trembling that resulted caused the church's closet shelves to collapse onto Chrisette. Darryl Junior dove deep into the filth of dirt, tools, and other miscellaneous church belongings to find Chrisette. Seeing Chrisette unconscious and covered with dirt and blood nearly drove my cousin insane. It was in that moment that he realized, more so than ever before, that she was indeed his soul mate. Darryl Junior sat by her side for the entire ambulance ride to the hospital. He prayed over her body, begging God for her recuperation. Tear drops fell from his eyes. He would have given anything to hear her voice again, so you can imagine his elation when her eyes slowly opened.

Through weak and low-hanging eye lids, Chrisette gazed into Darryl Junior's weeping face. She squeezed his hand as tightly as she could with her fatigued muscles. Her lips parted, but only breathe left them as she attempted to speak.

"Save your strength, Chrissy." Darryl Junior smiled with the relief that she would be okay.

"I love you." Chrisette struggled to speak with a soft but hoarse whisper before again falling asleep.

Chrisette slept with only the sound of the heart monitor to accompany her breathing. Darryl Junior could not remove her from his stare. She was his everything and he didn't want to live another moment without her by his side. As the sun slowly crept over the horizon, Darryl Junior realized that he was more than ready to make Chrisette his wife.

"Oh, Darryl Junior, I think that is a marvelous idea," Sister Emmagene gushed while jumping into my cousin's arms. Darryl Junior had just told Aunt HoneyBea of his plans to marry Chrisette, but before Aunt HoneyBea could react, Sister Emmagene quickly stole the moment.

"Excuse me Emmagene, but do you mind if I talk to my nephew for a moment?" Aunt HoneyBea rolled her eyes at Sister Emmagene.

"Of course. Talk away. I'm so excited. You've got to let me help with the wedding," Sister Emmagene continued.

"I haven't even asked her yet," Darryl Junior chuckled before Aunt HoneyBea nudged Sister Emmagene signaling her to move aside.

"Emmagene, when I asked could I speak with my nephew, I meant alone." Aunt HoneyBea forced as broad a smile as she could.

"Oh. Silly me. I'll be down the hall at the vending machines," Sister Emmagene said while finally prancing away.

"Darryl Junior, I'm so proud of you baby. I see the way you look at her and I recognize the way she looks at you. It's the same look I used to give your Uncle Tony P. Believe it or not, he was such a handsome man before the alcohol and hard life of gambling got a hold of him.

I loved that man so much. There was nothing that I wouldn't do to wake up as his wife every single morning of my life. When you feel that type of love, you have to hold on to it. Do right by that girl, Junior. Do right by her and I promise that she will always be a blessing to you." Aunt HoneyBea spoke with so much emotion as she contemplated on her early years with Uncle Tony P. She was so happy to see that Darryl Junior was growing into the kind of man who could provide that level of happiness to a woman.

"Thank you Aunty." Darryl Junior hugged Aunt HoneyBea as her tears of joy fell onto his shoulders.

Darryl Junior wanted the moment of his proposal to be extra special. He dressed in his best double-breasted, tailor-made suit. He bought a beautiful diamond ring and arranged for Chrisette's hospital room to be covered with roses, tulips, and hydrangeas. When she finally opened her eyes to the morning light, Darryl Junior knelt down beside her bed with the opened ring box extended before her face. Chrisette's eyes were fully alert as she took in the sight of the glistening diamond.

"Darryl, what the hell are you doing?" Chrisette screamed. Behind Darryl Junior, she could see a gang of people that Sister Emmagene had collected while prematurely shouting the news of their engagement through the streets of Hurley.

"I'm trying to propose to you. This isn't exactly the reaction that I was expecting." Darryl Junior laughed at the look of surprise growing on Chrisette's face.

"Darryl, no. Why would you do this? The last time we spoke, we were arguing. How did you get here from there?" Chrisette whispered to Darryl Junior so that none of the spectators could hear.

"You told me you loved me last night in the ambulance." Darryl said finally realizing that Chrisette's shocked disposition was not one of pleasure. Before Chrisette could respond, her four older brothers came pushing their way into the hospital room.

"C'mon, Chrissy, we've already filled out the paperwork for your discharge. Time to go." Her oldest brother, Damon, spoke.

"Wait a damn minute. Where did they come from? Chrissy, what's going on?" Darryl Junior exclaimed.

"I'm sorry, Darryl. I didn't want to hurt you. It's just that I was still so angry from our argument. I had the nurses contact my father early this morning," Chrisette tried to explain.

"But you said you loved me in the ambulance," Darryl Junior said.

"They had me on painkillers. I don't even remember saying that," Chrisette cried. "Darryl, I'm so sorry."

"Chrissy, come on. We ain't got time for this." Damon pushed his way past Darryl Junior.

"Hold up bruh. Can't you see we are talking?" Darryl Junior shoved Damon in retaliation. Damon quickly swung his right fist into Darryl Junior's jaw. My cousin dropped like a sack of potatoes.

"Damon, no. Get off him," Chrisette screamed.

"Get Chrissy out of here. We're going home." Damon ordered his brothers to grab Chrisette.

"Let me go," Chrissy screamed.

"Get off my nephew, you dumb heathen," Aunt HoneyBea screamed while swinging her purse at Damon.

"Don't worry, old lady. I'm leaving." Damon disrespectfully smirked before walking out of the hospital room.

Darryl Junior tried to get up and chase after them, but Aunt HoneyBea held him down. "Calm down baby. She'll come back."

Two days had passed and Friday morning found Darryl Junior with no call or visit from Chrisette. With a bruised face and a broken heart, my cousin had changed. He was no longer the suave and charming gentlemen that we had come to love. He became angry. He held little control over his temper and even the slightest things would set him off; so you can imagine that, with a house full of guests, his rage became a bit of a problem.

"Why are all these lights on? And who put all these toys on the floor? It looks like a freaking amusement park in here." Darryl Junior stood in the doorway to the basement, fuming with a small squeaky toy in his hands.

"There's my ducky. Hey Ducky. I missed you!" Ashley exclaimed while racing towards Darryl Junior.

"I almost broke my ankle on this stupid thing." Darryl Junior's anger could be seen as his veins protruded from his strong arms. His flexing arms tightened as he squeezed harshly against the small rubber toy. We all watched as his grip continued to tense until the small, rubber duck popped and exploded in his hand.

"Nooo. You killed ducky," Ashley screamed and cried while attending to her ruptured, rubber ducky.

"Man, what's wrong with you? You broke my sister's toy." Cora glared at Darryl Junior with the meanest pair of eyes.

"Darryl Junior, chill. They're just kids cuz." Cousin JuneBug rushed out of the basement as all the commotion erupted.

"Somebody better get these little bad ass kids before I perform a couple of post-op abortions in this piece," Darryl Junior yelled.

"Darryl Junior, what is all this noise about?" Aunt HoneyBea stormed out of the kitchen.

"Ashley, oh my God. Why is mama's baby crying?" Sister Emmagene came running behind her.

"There are toys all over the basement. I tripped on that stupid duck for the last time. When are they leaving?" Darryl Junior continued to express his rage.

"If you would look where you were going, you wouldn't trip. You're paying for my sister's duck, punk," Cora retorted and her statement set off an argument full of incoherent yelling.

"Everybody quiet," Aunt HoneyBea screamed at the top of her lungs. The entire house went silent. "Today is my baby sister's funeral. We're going to honor her memory. If it's nothing nice about Alieza Arden then I don't want to hear it. Is that clear?"

"But Auntie." Darryl Junior exclaimed.

"Boy, don't make me lose my religion in here today. I said, is that clear?" Aunt HoneyBea continued.

"It's clear." Everyone agreed as the house again fell into silence.

Silence dominated the rest of that afternoon as everyone prepared for the funeral. No one said anything. They were all unsure of what to say. To them, I was like a tiny, cracked glass figurine. One wrong word and they were sure I would shatter into tiny, unfixable pieces of devastation. Everyone, except for me, dressed in their finest black attire. I couldn't force myself to add another level of darkness to my already dimming life. I needed to feel my mother's light just one more time, even if it was just another lie. I searched through my closet and pulled out the white, satin floral gown that my mother had worn as a child. The floral patterns seemed to glisten beneath that afternoon's sunlight. I had worn the dress so many times before, but that day was different. Everyone looked upon me as If I was her ghost. I was the shining memory of a past innocence that she had long ago left behind. Even Aunt HoneyBea, who was normally strict about traditions, smiled after seeing me in the gown. I represented everything that she felt was lost to her baby sister after a life long battle with lies and mistakes.

An image of my mother's smiling face encircled by beautiful flowers was the first sight I remember seeing after walking into the church sanctuary. All eyes turned to take in the sight of the motherless child wearing white as I slowly entered the church. There was sadness in the room, but most of their minds were filled with judgment. I could see their thoughts through their stares. They were thinking of what a terrible mother she must've been to have left me alone. They were speculating on her whereabouts for all those years. Their minds were lost to gossip and rumors while my mind was left with the painful realization that my mother would forever be remembered as a lie.

Deacon Booker delivered the sermon in Pastor Bernard's absence. I hadn't heard from or seen Pastor Bernard since the hurricane. According to Sister Emmagene, no one had. The rumor around the city was that he'd completely lost his mind. Without the Pastor's presence in the sanctuary, the service seemed to drag along endlessly. The mood was dull and full of sorrow. There was no enthusiasm to distract me from the pain. I couldn't squeeze my scars with Aunt HoneyBea's eyes closely watching my every move. The moment quickly became overwhelming. My head grew light with each second. My pulse pounded from within me. Sweat beads flowed down my face as an inner heat burned within me. My nerves were on edge and my thoughts were scrambled with chaos. It was as if every emotion I had ignored since my mother left me eight years ago erupted all at once. I inhaled deeply, but my lungs burned as if no air was reaching them. I heaved with panic while struggling to breathe.

"Rumor, baby, what's wrong?" Aunt HoneyBea cried out as the low hum of the church organ was immediately replaced by my multiple gasps for air. I could find no air to speak. I heaved one last time as the room around me started to blur. "Somebody call a doctor."

The gradual leak of dripping water was the first sound I remembered hearing. Then all at once there was the rush of air entering my body. That first conscious breathe sounded as if a storm of wind entered me all at once. Then there was an overwhelming bright light. Was I dead? Before I could answer my own question, the light was quickly pushed aside.

The singing of a very familiar voice met my ears, "This old man seen plenty of kids. This old man seen plenty of roaches. Kids and roaches . . ."

"Old Man Pete? What are you doing here?" I squinted as the light of Old Man Pete's flashlight slowly dimmed from sight. It was just he and I alone in the damaged remains of the Church's dining hall.

"I'm working. What's it look like I'm doing? You chillens kill me. The church needed somebody to repaint these old, water-damaged walls," Old Man Pete grumbled.

"Ok, so why am I here?" I asked.

"Well as much as I hate you kids, and everybody knows that I hate you chillen, I must say that this old man had a soft spot for that Alieza Arden." Old Man Pete's usual frown slumped into a depressing pout.

"What do you know about my mother?"

"I know you chillen may find this hard to believe, but Old Man Pete been working for the Hurley School system for about 20 years now. Yeah, 20 long, long, long years. I've seen way too many of you bad-ass kids over these years. I mean rude ones, nasty ones, fat ones, and just plain ugly ones, but that Alieza was the sweetest lil thang I ever seen. She was a small girl. Just about your size. Those pretty brown eyes looked as big as the moon from behind those thick glasses that girl used to wear. I mean those were some thick glasses. First time I saw them big old thangs, I damn near crapped my pants. They looked like God's all-seeing eyes coming down to judge Old Pete." For the first time ever, I watched Old Man Pete smile at something other than the misery of someone's child.

"I get the point, Mr. Pete?"

"Watch yo' mouf, lil girl. Old man Pete don't take no talk-back. Lil nasty chillen get smacked-back when they be on that talk-back." Pete's face once again frowned. "Nah as weird as that lil girl looked; she was about as sweet as a strawberry. She was way too sweet to be around those lil menaces to society at that school. They teased and bullied that child like there was no tomorrow; and then when tomorrow came, they teased and bullied her some more. But this old man saw the smile behind that mouf full of metal. I kept watch over that child for as long as I could. I tried to protect her innocence, but there was nothing I could do to protect her from the one weakness of all lil girls."

"What was that?"

"Lil boys. That girl got all googly eyed for this one lil boy. What was that little bastard's name? Luxury, Lemon, Laughy, or some mess like that. She changed for that lil boy. The sweetest thang I ever seen changed for some lil heathen. She was never the same. The glasses came off, her skin cleared, and them braces were removed. She found womanhood in the worst way possible. This city chewed that lil girl up and spit her out as a downtrodden mess."

"What did they do to her? What happened to my mama?" I shouted as mountains of emotions grew within my heart.

"Sssh. Be quiet lil lady. You can't tell nobody I'm showing you this. I mean that now. I need this here gig. Only reason I'm doing this is because I miss that lil' sweet thang. The closest I've ever come to seeing her since she left town is when I would see your smiling face. You look so much like her. You ain't as sweet, but you look so much like her."

"What are you showing me?"

"Just look up at the wall, child. I removed all that wet plaster and dry wall and look what I found underneath it." Old Man Pete pointed upwards.

I followed the trail of his finger to one of the most gorgeous sights I'd ever laid eyes on. It was a large, colorfully painted mural. The beautiful painting spread from one corner of the wall to the next. There were gorgeous butterflies painted with bright purples, reds, greens, yellows, and all sorts of amazing color combinations. Tall stalks of green grass grew throughout the painting. Various shades of color were splattered across the top to represent the shades of light that dominated the day. The center of the mural was decorated with a smiling woman. Her long flowing hair was a dark shade of blue. Her smiling face was made of glistening purple. She wore a long, flowing sundress painted with all sorts of colors. In her arms, she held a baby. Her eyes and the baby's eyes were angled to directly face one another. Even through the painting, her love for that child was overwhelmingly clear. Beside her was the black shadow of a man. He seemed as if he were the missing piece to their gorgeous family puzzle.

"Amazing. Who did this?"

"Your mother did this. It was so long ago I'd forgotten about it. I'm sure most of the city forgot. That's what they wanted. That's why they covered it up; but to me, the most beautiful thing about this painting is that in it I see that lil girl. That lil girl they thought they had destroyed was still alive. She was very much alive and it showed on the walls of the church. She painted this entire mural with berries. Nothing but crushed berries. She mashed each berry with her own hands and wiped her emotions across this wall. Your mama had a gift lil girl. She had an amazing gift. She had a light that wouldn't dim and she passed that light on to you. Don't you ever let that light go out."

I couldn't remove my eyes from the stunning mural. My mother was more than a crafter of words or an architect of beautiful, tall tales. She was the creator of gorgeous truths, and her greatest truth was evident through her love for me.

"Rumor," Aunt HoneyBea's voice echoed down the halls of the church.

"Get back in there, girl. They can't know that you saw this mural or it's the long lines of unemployment for Old Pete." Old Man Pete warned.

"Thank you Mr. Pete." I rushed Old Man Pete with the tightest hug that I could muster and planted a kiss on his left cheek.

"I said get out of here nah, girl. Don't be on me with all that mushy mess. Get out of here." Old Man Pete yelled, but I swear as I raced out of there I could see his cheeks swelling with happiness. He wasn't as mean as he wanted people to believe.

As I quietly made my way back into the church, Aunt HoneyBea found me tip-toeing slowly down the hallway. She released a heavy sigh of relief. "Rumor, where have you been? I've been looking all over this church for you, girl. I go to find you a glass of water and you just disappeared on me."

"I'm fine, Auntie. I just had to use the restroom," I lied.

"Baby, you gotta stop scaring me like this. My old heart can't take too much more," Aunt HoneyBea said.

"I'm sorry, Auntie."

"It's okay, baby. You've been through a lot. Do you think you can handle seeing her buried? If not, you know you don't have to go."

"I know, but I need to go . . . for her." I smiled, but behind that smile my mind was moving at a rate of hundreds of miles per minute. I needed to figure out the identity of the shadow man in the mural. He had to be the key to the truth. Miss Tuna said the truth lay behind only one face. I couldn't help but think that maybe that face belonged to the man who was missing from my mother's mural.

The flowers of spring blossomed beautifully across the sacred land of the cemetery. We passed rows of tombstones on our way to my mother's burial site. Each one marked the remains of brothers, sisters, fathers, mothers, and friends. Each one marked a hole in the beating heart of someone's living relative, a hole similar to the one that had been torn into my own heart. If their pain was anything close to what I'd been feeling, I pitied them all. In that moment, I even found pity for the Tahiri triplets who stood beneath a tent on the other side of the cemetery weeping for the death of their brother.

Minutes later, we all stood facing my mother's casket. I had no more tears to shed as Deacon Booker said a final prayer over her body. In my mind, all I could see was the shadowy figure in my mother's mural. We were all so quiet that the sound of crunching leaves seemed to crash like thunder. My eyes followed the sound of a man slowly walking towards the burial site. The bright afternoon sun eclipsed his image. As he continued to approach us, he was nothing but a shadow. He was the same shadow from my mother's mural. It was as if God instantly answered my prayer. There he was approaching me. Sure that I had to be dreaming, I blinked repeatedly to focus my mind; but the shadow man continued to approach. He was real. As he stepped into sight, it became clear that he was Pastor Bernard.

"Oh my God, Beatrice, look." Sister Emmagene looked down at me while excitedly whispering to my Auntie.

"Oh, no. Rumor, baby, it's time for us to go." Aunt HoneyBea quickly grabbed my hand to guide me away from the burial grounds, but I couldn't leave.

It was Pastor Bernard who stood before me as the mystery man in my mother's mural. I had so many questions to ask him. I yanked free of my aunt's grip as I continued to gaze into Pastor Bernard's direction. As he returned my stare, his eyes immediately dropped down to my dress. Suddenly I felt the stares of everyone on my dress. I looked down at a large, blood-red stain spreading across the lower part of my white gown. On that day, I became a woman.

Rumor's Journal (Entry 7)

Crushed berry juices dripping all around me,
Waves in a sea of stares, blinding them completely.
There they go as they look from around me
trying to figure out what's happening inside me
They hear my heart beating,
but they can't provide my healing,
as they try to look through and see the pain that I'm
concealing.
The truth of the matter: They'll never know what I'm
feeling.

Chapter 8

Truth Eruption

I have so many aunts, but no one warned me about old Aunt Flo. That's what I remember Sister Emmagene calling it anyway. It was one of the most embarrassing moments of my life. As they lowered my mother six feet to a point of no return, the beautiful dress that had so many times reminded me of her presence was left ruined as well. The blood of my womanhood had spread across the floral patterns giving them the appearance of blossoming roses. Pastor Bernard, the man who undoubtedly held the answers to so many of my questions, stood wide eyed and speechless as Aunt HoneyBea hauled me away in her car.

Later that evening, I sat quietly soaking in warm bath water. By the looks of my wrinkling skin, I must have sat in that bathtub for hours. I felt so filthy. It was as if there was a stain that I could not rub off. I could no longer feel the innocence of childhood, but the independence of womanhood was still too far away. The only thing I could do was study my own face as the bath water reflected my image. I looked the same; however, I appeared nearly unrecognizable. I didn't know the girl who returned my stare. At that point, I wasn't sure if I had ever known her.

The house phone rang loudly from outside the bathroom. I could hear Aunt HoneyBea as she answered it. The elevated and operatic tone of her voice was one of excitement. "Oh yes. That is great news. I can't wait to tell Rumor. My poor baby needs to hear some good news."

I couldn't even imagine anything making me feel better at that moment. There was a hole within me, a giant gap that no one could fill. I glanced over at my bandaged arm which hung out over the side of the bathtub. Gia's pink razor, which she used to shave her legs, lay on the other side of the tub near the wall. I needed more pain but unfortunately my arm wound was quickly healing. The sight of blood had become the norm for me, and I imagined the blade of the razor piercing my freshly healed skin. In my mind I could see rivers of blood flowing from my arms into the bath water. I grabbed the razor. Its blades shined beneath the light of the bathroom. I could see the unrecognizable reflection of my face on the blade's small surface. I hated the girl that I saw. I hated her because she was weak and pathetic; but most of all, I hated her because I did not know her.

"Rumor." Aunt HoneyBea knocked against the bathroom door. Her unexpected knock startled me causing me to drop the razor down into the water beneath me.

"Yes," I answered with a slightly shaken voice. My nerves were still on edge from the thoughts of self-hatred that dominated my mind.

"Taylor's awake. I'm taking you to the hospital in the morning. Louise says he won't stop asking about you." She was excited as she broke the news to me, but I didn't know how to feel. I was relieved that Taylor was doing better. I just wasn't sure that I wanted him to see the girl in my reflections. She was not the girl he would remember. She was not even worthy of his friendship.

The next morning, Aunt HoneyBea cooked a big breakfast of eggs, grits, bacon, sausage, and French toast for the entire house. The aroma of freshly cooked meat and cinnamon sweetened bread revived me from Friday night's slumber. I hadn't eaten much over those last few days, so the smell awakened a beastly rumble from within my stomach. As hungry as I was, amazingly I still had to battle my nerves to eat. It felt like years since I'd last seen Taylor. So many things had changed. I wasn't even sure what we would talk about or how he'd look after having been hit by a pickup truck.

"Eat up Rumor. We've gotta be at the hospital by 9. Louise says the nurses are being real strict about Taylor's visiting hours." Aunt HoneyBea gushed with enthusiasm.

"I'm done," I replied after only a few bites. The breakfast was incredible, but the effort of each bite as I fought against my nerves was too much.

"You barely touched your plate. You usually love my French toast." Aunt HoneyBea looked at my plate with confusion.

"I'll just save it for later, Auntie. I'm going to start getting ready." I pushed away from the table and hurried back to my room. Everyone but Aunt HoneyBea barely even noticed me as they chomped away at their breakfast.

When I entered our bedroom, Gia lay soundly asleep, as usual, beneath the covers of her bed. She shifted slightly as the hallway light shone across her bed. Careful not to wake her, I slowly closed the door behind me. No one bothered Gia. She had been through so much. Everyone assumed the baby that she'd miscarried was fathered by her boyfriend, K. Mack. No one even suspected that Deputy Ron Mack may have been the father. Only Deputy Ron and I knew that, and neither of us was saying anything. Since the accident, Gia's cell phone rang every hour with a call from either K. Mack or Deputy Ron. She never answered. K Mack, who knew nothing about the baby before the accident, made every attempt to see her, but Gia constantly refused his company. She shut every one out. Even her best friend, Princess, found it hard to capture my cousin's attention. Gia had become a recluse.

I tip toed across the bedroom to my closet. As I pulled open the door, the hinges creaked loudly. I glanced back at Gia hoping I hadn't awakened her. As she sat upwards free from her covers, I knew it was too late. Her eyes were red, puffy, and swollen from so many days of endless sleep and tears. Her hair was wild and nappy as it spread out all over her head. As rough as she appeared, it was the defeated look in her eyes that gave me the most chills.

"I'm sorry, Gia," I whispered hoping not to catch the worst of Gia's wrath.

"What time is it?" she asked after a series of tired groans.

"It's 7:30. Go back to sleep. I didn't mean to wake you," I replied.

"You didn't mean to wake me? Rumor, why do you even care that you woke me up? I promise I don't understand you," Gia said while wiping the crust from her eyes.

"What do you mean?" I asked.

"I've always been such a bitch to you. Hell, I'm mean to everyone. Why do you care about me? Why do you tip toe around here trying not to set me off? Someone needs to set me off. I deserve everything that has happened to me and so much more. I hate myself and I wait for everyone else to hate me too, but all I get is pity." Tears fell from Gia's tired eyes as she spoke.

"Gia don't say that. No one deserves the stuff that's happened to you."

"Don't humor me, Rumor. I was pregnant and I have no idea who was my baby's daddy. I cheated on my boyfriend and fell in love with his brother. I was so foolish. I seduced him, Rumor. He turned me down so many times. Ron warned me that it was not right for us to be together, but I wouldn't listen. I just had to have him. I had to have him so bad that I may have ruined his life for my own selfish emotions."

"Gia, no one knows about you and Ron, and no one is going to find out."

"Let's be real here, Cousin. Lies never stay hidden. You, of all people, should know that. Lies came back and killed your mother; and as much as I want to believe that I'm somehow different, I'm not. My life is just like your mother's. Hell, my life is worse. I killed my child."

"You didn't kill your baby. It was an accident."

"I wanted it dead, Rumor. I prayed for its death. I went to that old woman for an abortion. She was going to sell me herbs to help abort my child. I wanted that abortion so bad that I was willing to sell my dead mama's ring for it. I may as well have punched myself in the stomach. Don't pity me, Rumor. I don't deserve your pity. Hate me because I'm ten times worse than the woman who abandoned you." Gia sunk down low into her bed and again covered herself with her bed linens.

I didn't know what to say to her. Lies had destroyed my mother, but they were not all lies that she, herself, had told. I was sure that most of the lies were still being told.

As much as I wanted to help Gia, I couldn't. I couldn't help her find her truth because I still had to find my own.

I felt the impact of Gia's words for the rest of that day. Even during the walk down the hospital's hallways, I could still hear her speaking. Why was I always so kind to Gia when she always treated me so disrespectfully? After a few lies, I couldn't contain my anger towards my mother, but when it came to Gia, I could never hold a grudge. Maybe subconsciously Gia represented my truth. Even when I had no idea that I was surrounded by lies, Gia was always the most obvious truth.

As I darkened the doorway to Taylor's room, my thoughts finally eased at the sight of his dimpled smile. All of my worries about seeing him again, about Gia, or even about my mother faded under the brightness of Taylor's light. Before I realized it, I had run to his bed and squeeze him with the tightest hug.

"Be careful, Rumor. He's still healing," Aunt HoneyBea said.

"I'm okay . . . Rumor, what took you so long to get here? It feels so good to see the familiar face of someone not wearing a white coat. I swear if I see one more white coat, it'll be from inside those padded walls," Taylor joked. He was always so positive even in the midst of the most negative situations. I hadn't realized just how much I missed him until that moment.

"I'm here now, Homie." I continued to squeeze him tightly as a tear drop of joy fell down my cheek.

Aunt HoneyBea and Louise left us alone as we talked for hours about any and everything. Our conversations were so effortless and refreshing. I avoided mentioning Manny because I was sure that was a topic neither of us wanted to touch. Nothing else was off limits. Taylor's left leg was in a cast and hoisted above him, preventing him from going anywhere. With him and me together, his physical limitations didn't matter. Our minds were like large clouds of pure imagination.

We envisioned ourselves aboard giant rafts floating down the Nile River. The moon was large and the ancient sky was littered with many stars. The reflection of each star seemed to dance across the surface of the rippling river. We were surrounded by jungle trees. Long, thin tree trunks grew high above us on all sides. Tree branches, holding giant, green leaves and delicious fruits, extended over us. Playful monkeys laughed while swinging from branch to branch. Birds sung in unison, leading the natural choir. Crickets, snakes, wild cats, and many other jungle animals lifted our spirits with the hymns of the heavens.

I was Queen Cleopatra and Taylor was the Roman general Marcus Antonius. It was his first exhibition into the heart of Africa, and I served as his personal tour guide throughout the magnificent mother land. Together we marveled at the beauty of the mineral enriched land. The winds guided our navigation as we sailed from the shores of Egypt to that of Southern Sudan. Taylor stood in awe at the jewels and fine cloth that adorned me, the

Queen of the Nile. I couldn't help but be impressed by his royal stature and perfectly molded weaponry. In our imaginations, we were visions of perfection. He was the cure to my sorrow and I was the end of his suffering. We completed one another in the most magical way.

Our pupils reflected the beauty of the Nile from the innermost depths of our imaginations, but a plain, white hospital room surrounded us on all sides. I focused on his eyes and he focused on mine as we were lost to the beautiful African lands that our minds had concocted. After being best friends for so many years, Taylor and I had imagined many things together, but something was different about that time. I felt something that I had never felt before. There was a longing growing inside of me. It was a longing for closer intimacy. I felt safe with Taylor, safer than I had felt in a long time. Cleopatra's lips pouted as the winds of Africa guided her into the arms of her Marcus Antonius. I was overwhelmed by the fantasy, and before I could regain my senses, I had already planted a gentle kiss onto Taylor's unsuspecting lips.

"Woah. What are you doing?" Taylor stared at me through rounded eyes and with a dropped jaw.

"Oh my God. I'm sorry, Taylor. I got carried away." My cheeks burned red with embarrassment. I couldn't believe I had just kissed my best friend on the lips. I wanted to take that moment back so badly. Every part of me told me to run, but my legs would not move.

"Chill out, Rumor. I'm not trippin'. It was Cleopatra who kissed Marc Antony. It wasn't us, right?" Taylor chuckled before inquiring into the reason behind the kiss. I didn't know what to say. I couldn't tell him that newfound woman within me desired it. I couldn't confess that it was me. He was my best friend and I was ashamed of wanting him, even if just for a second.

"Yeah. Of course. You didn't think it was me, did you? I mean, c'mon Taylor, we're like brother and sister. Ugh. That's nasty," I lied.

"That's what I thought. Rumor, there's something I have to tell you before our parents come back." Taylor's expression quickly turned serious.

"What is it? Taylor, you know that you can tell me anything," I said.

"I've been debating on whether or not I was going to say anything," Taylor said.

"What's going on?" I asked.

Taylor sighed deeply before he continued. "I came out of my coma a lot sooner than I'm leading everyone to believe that I did. At first I was just too weak to say anything, but after I opened my eyes I saw my mother talking to an older man. Apparently, he was my grandfather. I didn't even know that I had a grandfather. I mean, of course, everyone does, but my mother never brought him up before. I just assumed that he was dead or something."

"I'm confused, Taylor. Why wouldn't you want to tell me that?"

"Because there's more," Taylor continued. "My mother seemed to be very upset as they spoke. She was crying and everything. It wasn't long before I found out why."

"Yeah?" I urged him to proceed.

"Well, from what I overheard, it sounds like your mother didn't leave Hurley by choice."

"What?" My voice was beginning to crack with nervous intensity.

"Promise me you won't get mad. I don't want to start any trouble, Rumor. I just felt like, as your best friend, I owed you to tell you."

"Taylor, I'm fine. Just tell me what you heard already."

"It was the church. They labeled her as a whore and forced her to leave the city." Taylor's head dropped as he spoke.

"How could they force her to leave the city? It doesn't make any sense. How could they force her to leave me?" I cried.

"She left for you. You know how it is in Hurley. The church controls everything. They had already outcast her and made her life hell. They were promising to do the same to you. No school would accept you. No other child would play with you. You would be labeled as the daughter of a whore. She didn't want to take you with her because she was still so young. She knew she wouldn't be able to give you the life you deserved, so she left you with your Aunt HoneyBea."

"No. It can't be true. Why would they do that to her? It's the church. Everyone's welcome in the church. Pastor

Bernard says that all the time. Why would he . . ." As I spoke, I remembered the mural. I recalled the image of the shadow man and how much he resembled Pastor Bernard. I fell silent.

"Rumor, are you okay?" Taylor asked as I stood quietly pondering on my thoughts.

"How does your grandfather know so much about my mother?" I asked.

"That's the part that I really didn't want to go into," Taylor sighed.

"You mean to tell me that it gets worse!" I exclaimed.

"He found her on the streets of Biloxi. She was starving, homeless, and lonely. A few more days on her own, and she would've died out there. He took her in and gave her a job."

"A job doing what?" I inquired.

"He prostituted her. Rumor, I'm sorry." Taylor reached out to comfort me with a hug, but I quickly dodged his arm. I backed away from his reach with sheer shock on my face. Gia's words from earlier returned to my thoughts. Lies never stay hidden. They had all fooled me. Her death was no longer an accident in my mind. My mother was murdered. Gia was right. Lies had killed her. Hurley's lies killed her. The church's lies buried her. My family's lies caused us to forget her. The last week had revealed a mountain of betrayal, but that day the mountain was volcanic. The truth was about to erupt all over the city of Hurley.

"Okay, Rumor, time's up. The doctor says Taylor needs his rest." Aunt HoneyBea came prancing in, completely unaware of the bomb of truth that had just been dropped onto me.

Rumor's Journal (Entry 8)

When you're a child all you know
is a bunch of tall tales,
Like how Jack and Jill fetched a certain pail,
Or how humpty dumpty cracked his little shell.
It's the little lies that will always dwell,
At first so sweet until expiration brings a smell,
A rotten aroma that leaves a fowl taste,
Tales molded into lies so putrid that all innocence goes
to waste.

Chapter 9

Kingdom Church

For so long, the church has been the back bone to so many Black-American communities. Church is where we find our healing, our fellowship, our leisure, our work, our love, our wisdom, and so much more. Church worship was the only thing that maintained us throughout so many years of slavery and discrimination. We found comfort in God's house. It's always been the pillow of comfort to a people aching through years of oppression. Because of the church's many benefits to our lives, it's never been a problem to yield absolute power over the community to the leaders of the church. It's the one organization that we've always been able to blindly trust; but unfortunately, where there is man, there is always corruption.

The Rock of the Delta First Missionary Baptist Church in our small town of Hurley, Mississippi, was no different. Pastor Bernard Johnson inherited the church from his deceased father, Reverend Oscar Johnson. Under Bernard Johnson, the church flourished into a powerful business entity that single handedly maintained Hurley. It was the church that negotiated the deal with Nelson Paper Company to provide jobs to citizens of Hurley. It was also the church that had procured the grant to build Mercy Projects to house the poor citizens of Hurley.

Pastor Bernard Johnson had become a symbol of hope for the city. He was their hero, but with rumors of his insanity running rampant across the city, people were beginning to panic. News of a murder, widespread damage from a natural disaster, and the possible closing of Nelson Paper Company left the citizens of Hurley desperate for a hero, but Pastor Bernard was nowhere to be found.

"I've requested the presence of all of you here today because as leaders of the church, you are all pillars to this community. I'm sure you have all watched the news. Everything is falling apart. We need the church to intervene." Deputy Mayor Sheila Owen stood before the counsel of church leaders pleading for their help.

"If everything is so bad, where is the mayor? Why isn't he here talking to us, himself?" Sister Janice leaned back and folded her arms with a demeanor of disapproval.

"That's a good question? Where is he?" Deacon Hamilton asked.

"I assure you all that he wanted to be here himself, but he had a very important meeting with the Governor this afternoon."

"Mmm hmm, more like a very important meeting with a bottle of Wild Irish Rose." Sister Mary Gibson flicked her Chinese fan into the air, waving a fresh breeze of wind through her synthetic hair. Mayor Clarke's alleged alcohol infused antics were always the talk of the town, and Sister Mary Gibson was never one to shy away from good gossip.

"C'mon everybody, cool down. Let's hear what Ms. Owen has to say. After all, we are the leaders of this community." Deacon Booker stood from his seat and walked to the head of the table beside Deputy Mayor Owen.

"Thank you, Deacon," Deputy Mayor Owen smiled with a slight sign of blushing. "I was hoping that the church could spearhead a couple of fundraisers and take up a few offerings to save the city's budget."

"Oh, so we are supposed to break our backs out here raising money for some corrupt city officials? No ma'am," Sister Janice quickly spoke.

"Ms. Janice, these fundraisers will benefit the entire city of Hurley and the mayor's office will provide all of the assistance that the church could possibly need. This is a win-win situation for all," Deputy Mayor Owen pled to the counsel.

"Look, Miss Owen, this church is not about to sit here and help bail that incompetent old drunk out of another situation, and I mean that," Sister Janice snapped.

"My apologies, Janice. I guess I just assumed that with a pastor who's half out of his mind and running around the city making a fool of himself, this church of all places would understand." Deputy Mayor Owen could no longer hide the irritation that was building inside of her from the debate with Sister Janice.

"Now ladies, we're going to remain respectable, right?" Deacon Booker attempted to intervene as the tension in the room continued to elevate.

"You'd better get her. I don't care who she works for her. I ain't the one." Sister Janice immediately stood to her feet.

"Janice, have a seat." First Lady Silvia, who sat quietly throughout the meeting, finally spoke.

"Thank you, Silvia," Deputy Mayor Owen said.

"Don't thank me, because my husband's church will not be doing any fund raisers for the mayor's office," First Lady Silvia retorted.

"Well, I don't think it's a bad idea," Deacon Booker said.

"No. Not a bad idea. Just a foolish one," First Lady Silvia continued. "We're going to campaign to a poor town full of poor citizens for money to fill the poor budget. That doesn't make any sense."

"Then, with all due respect, may I ask what do you suggest?" Deputy Mayor Owen asked.

"I'm glad you asked. Although my husband is currently dealing with extreme personal issues, this church will not lose one step because he married a woman who truly knows how to cover her man's back. I have been negotiating a deal that will solve all of Hurley's problems."

"What kind of deal?" Deacon Hamilton inquired.

"I'll allow him to explain that part. Come in, Mr. Grimes." First Lady Silvia glanced at the door to their meeting room just as it swung open to reveal Caesar Grimes on the other end.

"Are you out of your mind? Why is he here?" Deacon Booker exclaimed.

"Silvia, you know I'm always here for you and the pastor, but this ain't making no sense. This man tried to kill your husband. Why is he in this church?" Sister Janice asked.

"Oooh, chile. This is better than watching my stories." Sister Mary Gibson's mouth dropped with excitement.

"Just hear the man out. Aren't we supposed to be Christian people?" First Lady Silvia replied.

"Thank you Silvia, but they are all entitled to their doubts. I am a man who understandably falls victim to his own reputation. I have done some terrible things in the past, but of all the evil that I am guilty of, my heart aches most when I think of what happened to Bernard Johnson." Caesar Grimes walked around the table maintaining eye contact with each person in the room as he spoke.

"I'm not listening to this mess. I grew up with Lucky, I mean Bernard. I remember what you did to him. He almost died in the E.R. a few times after you and your goons were done beating on him." Deacon Booker slammed his fist against the surface of the conference.

"Andrew Booker. You were a very smart young man. I remember reading my daughter's year book. They voted you most likely to succeed. Last I heard you were headed to some big time University in New York. I never imagined that you'd end up being Lucky's little side kick, so I'm sure that you, of all people, can understand that people do indeed change," Caesar Grimes suavely spoke.

"You know what old man? We ain't children no more. We can take this outside." Deacon Booker stood to his feet with anger in his eyes.

"As I said before, Andrew, I'm not here as the man of my past. I'm here as a man seeking forgiveness for his life's indiscretions."

"I know you, Caesar Grimes. You're nothing more than a low-life thug and there ain't no coming back for people like you," Deacon Booker said.

"Let he who is without sin cast the first stone." Caesar Grimes quoted the Bible with confidence.

"And just like the devil, he sure knows his Bible." Deacon Booker pushed against the table as he made his way towards Caesar.

"Deacon, go cool off. I'll handle things in here." Deacon Hamilton quickly grabbed Deacon Booker just as he was inches away from Caesar.

"I just wanna talk to him." Deacon Booker continued to reach for the man he viewed as his enemy.

"You're in the church, Andrew. Please, go cool off," Deacon Hamilton implored.

"Fine. If you wanna sit here and listen to this mess, be my guest. I'm out of here. I hope God protects your souls after whatever deal you all make with this demonic man," Deacon Booker said before pushing his way out of the conference room.

"Now that that little outburst is done, can we have a mature meeting like adults? What is wrong with you people? My husband has given his all for this city. He always put the needs of Hurley before his own. Don't you think that if this man has a way of saving this city that Bernard would sit here and at least hear him out?" First Lady Silvia attempted to calm some of the contempt growing within the room. The counsel stared at her with looks of confusion, but they calmly found their seats out of trust for their first lady.

"I'm going to keep this brief so as not to cause any further commotion. I've spoken to the Board of Directors at Nelson Paper, but they are adamant about moving their company to a larger market. However, we were able to reach a compromise. I'll provide the seed money to build a brand new, state—of—the—art casino complex right here in Hurley, Mississippi. Nelson Paper will provide their land for the location, and they've also agreed to financially contribute as silent partners in this venue. As a majority shareholder of Gulf Gamble stock, I can extend their business into the area as a franchise. The architecture has already been drawn and all paperwork has been submitted. This project is ready to go. All we need is the vote of the people to proceed," Caesar explained.

"This is a Christian town. We can't bring all that drunken debauchery into Hurley," Deacon Hamilton objected.

"Gulf Gamble states their net worth at nearly $10 billion dollars. If only a fraction of that money goes into this city, just imagine the improvements that we can bring to Hurley. Think about your communities. We can clean up Mercy Projects for good and make this city safe again. Think about your children and all the strides we can make in improving their education," Caesar continued.

"I'm sorry. I can't in good conscience stand behind this," Deacon Hamilton said.

"Well, I say we leave it up to the citizens of Hurley. All who are with us vote by a show of hands," First Lady Silvia added. She and Caesar were both pleased to see that every arm around the table rose, with the exception of Sister Janice and Deacon Hamilton.

"There you have it. Majority rules. We'll bring the casino vote before the citizens at tonight's Town Hall meeting. Thank you, Mr. Grimes," Deputy Mayor Owens concluded.

Town Halls were a pretty big deal in Hurley. They were like the big social event of each season. People dressed in their newest attire knowing that everyone who was anyone would be in attendance. Aunt HoneyBea and a few of the other church ladies would prepare their greatest dishes for a post-meeting potluck. After the disaster that was Hurricane Veronya, the people of Hurley needed a release from their own misery.

I, on the other hand, did not want a release from my misery. I needed to feel it. I needed to savor the fruits of everyone's deception. I didn't want to forget the pain, so I added to it. I looked down at my wrist wounds as they were still healing. Healing was a sign of moving on. I didn't want to move on. I felt that if I moved on, I'd be no different from the rest of Hurley. They destroyed my mother and moved on as if she never existed. I made up my mind that I would never move on. With the sharp blade of Aunt HoneyBea's kitchen knife pressed against my arm, I knew that relishing the pain was my only option.

Pastor Bernard, who was at wits end, was tired of moving past his problems, and he refused to continue and relish in them. He was determined that the only way he could regain his sanity was to face his issues head on. He stood facing the long hallway leading to the hospital's hospice unit. His heart pounded within his chest. At the end of that hallway, there was a room which held the one person that he'd always feared. Even in her condition of weakened health, her sphere of influence could still be felt in his every action. He needed to free himself of the past, and he knew that a conversation with his mother would be the best place to start.

Lula Mae Johnson had always been a powerful force in Hurley. During her term as the first lady of the church, Lula Mae easily commanded the respect and admiration of the people. She was more strong, intelligent, and elegant than anyone who had ever lived in the city of Hurley. In her mind, her family was royalty within the city. Her husband was the king and the church was his throne. Her son, Lucky, was set to inherit the throne, and she would do anything to ensure that he received his inheritance.

In public, Lula Mae was admirable. She held all the traits of a perfect mother and wife, but in private she was a terror. She expected Lucky to always be perfect. He had to have the best grades, the biggest smile, and the most polite manners of all the children. As the future Pastor of The Rock of the Delta First Missionary Baptist, he had to be well-liked amongst his subjects. If he ever fell short of perfection, her punishments were nothing short of abusive. Few people knew about the ferocious beatings dealt to Lucky at the hands of his mother. Even Lucky's father, the Reverend Oscar Johnson, would not dare to stop his son's torture as he also feared what his wife was truly capable of.

As Lucky grew older in age, Lula Mae knew that the beatings would no longer work as sufficient punishment for her teenage son. This is when true hell began for poor Lucky. If he ever stepped out of line, Lula Mae would lock him in the basement for hours at a time. Surrounded by roaches, rats, spiders, and dust, Lucky's mind reached towards delusions for normalcy and his secret battles with insanity started.

From that point on, there was only one person Lucky could trust to soothe the calamitous nature of his tortured soul. He had seen her many times around town. Her name was Alieza Arden. She was hardly noticeable as she walked quietly with her head always facing the ground. With thick bifocals and large metal braces, her appearance was very hard on the eyes, but there was something deeper within her that Lucky found attractive. He loved her for her words.

On one spring day while in a hurry to catch the bus after school, Alieza mistakenly dropped a small notepad on the ground. Lucky tried his best to capture her attention before she boarded the bus, but he was too late as they drove off into the sunset. The note pad was full of wonderful poetry. Her words were like small slices of heaven and his brain hungered for more. While reading her words, he never saw the false visions or heard any of the imagined voices. She dominated his mind and for the first time in years, through her, Lucky found peace.

The next day he returned the pad to her and they formed a genuine friendship. He, the perfect and popular senior, and she, the weird and awkward eighth grader, secretly became inseparable. His decision to hide their friendship was never one made out of shame, but it was to protect her. She was innocent and perfect. He never wanted her to know the hidden evils of his world, but it was only a matter of time before Lula Mae discovered their relationship.

Alieza grew to love Lucky more than he was aware. She was addicted to his time and attention. She started to notice the difference between the attention he gave her and the attention that he gave to the other girls, especially one girl in particular. At the time her name was Louise Grimes. She was the most beautiful girl Alieza had ever seen, and Alieza was determined to match her beauty in order to gain Lucky's affections. Over time, Alieza's braces came off, her acne cleared, and she switched from glasses to contact lenses. Her body developed into that of a woman's twice her age, and she proudly showcased her new look on stage at The Sweet Tea of the Delta Debutante Beauty Pageant. She could see by the look in Lucky's eyes that for the first time he saw her for more than just her words. Unfortunately for Lucky, Lula Mae could see his desire for the young Alieza as well.

Later that evening, Lucky slept in bed dreaming of the beautiful Alieza. He had not been able to free his mind of her since seeing her on stage. All he could think about was the splendor of her words magnified greatly by the loveliness of her looks. It was as if she had cast a spell of love. He wanted to see her so badly that he could no longer wait. He opened his eyes from sleeping hoping to find her, but instead he found the cold sensation of a steel blade pressed against his neck.

"I have sacrificed everything for you boy. How dare you embarrass me out there today as if I'm nobody to you?" Lula Mae stood above Lucky with her hands tightly gripping a large butcher knife.

"Mama, what are you talking about?" Lucky carefully spoke as the sharp end of the blade touched his skin.

"Don't play stupid with me, boy. I saw the way you looked at her. All of Hurley saw the way you looked at her. You will not tear down everything that I have built by getting caught up with some young, fast tail girl. Stay away from her, Lucky. I mean it. Stay away from her or I swear I'll kill you myself before I let you drag this family down into some scandal." The cold hard look in Lula Mae's eyes was a sure sign to Lucky that she was serious. His heart longed for Alieza, but his fear would not allow him to defy his mother.

As he took his first step down the hallway of the hospital's hospice unit, Pastor Bernard could not help but contemplate on the memory of his mother's threat. So many years had passed, but he could still feel the cold steel pressing against his throat. Even though she was now lying on her dying bed, her threat was still very much alive in his mind. "Stay away from her or I swear I'll kill you . . ."

A few minutes later, he stood before the doorway looking at the woman who had raised him. She looked nothing like the woman that she had been in her youth. She was thin and her skin was covered with wrinkles and liver spots. She breathed loudly into a machine as her eyes drooped around within their sockets. Her head was shaven bald after several treatments of chemotherapy had taken most of her hair. By the sight of her, it was hard to believe that anyone could still view her as a threat, but Pastor Bernard's heart sunk down into his shoes the moment their eyes met.

"Lucky, boy is that you?" She struggled to speak while removing the oxygen tube from her mouth.

"Yea, Mama, it's me," Pastor Bernard answered. Walking towards her, he still felt like that young boy from so long ago.

"Come closer, boy. My eyes ain't what they used to be," Lula Mae commanded.

"Hey Mama." His voice shook as he quietly addressed her.

"I thought I told you not to visit me here," Lula Mae snapped. "I told you I don't want anyone seeing me like this. What is wrong with you, boy? Can't an old lady just die in peace?"

"Mama, we're still praying to God for a healing miracle. You're gonna make it through this."

"Don't patronize me, boy. I'm practically dead already. Just get on with it. What do you want from me?"

"I just wanted to see you," Pastor Bernard said.

"Ain't nobody wanted to see me since your father died. Stop lying. What do you want?" Lula Mae retorted.

"I wanna talk," he confessed.

"Talk? About what?" Lula Mae exclaimed before bursting into a fit of coughs.

"Alieza Arden died a couple of days ago."

"Great. Good riddance. Now I know that ain't why you down here bothering me on my last days." Lula Mae continued to speak after taking a few breathes in her oxygen tube.

"Mama, stop being so hateful. You know how I felt about her." Pastor Bernard couldn't believe the hatred that was spewing out of her mouth. He expected that her heart would have at least softened a little bit on her death bed, but she was just as mean as she had always been. He was fed up with her bitter contempt for Alieza.

"Now we have the truth. That's why you really came down here. You wanna help put me in the grave a lil faster, because that's the only reason I can think of for you to come down here and rub this mess in my face."

"The truth? You wouldn't know the truth if you saw it, Mama."

"Boy, watch your mouth. I am still your mother."

"And I am a grown man," Pastor Bernard shouted. For the first time throughout their conversation, he did not feel like Lucky anymore. "I have to live with the lies that you forced me to tell for the rest of my life. I don't want to hear any complaints about your death bed. You have been slowly killing me since the day I was born. Thanks to you, I am dead inside."

"Thanks to me? You made your own bed, Bernard. I couldn't force you to do anything. Thank God I'm dying. I can't stand living and seeing the weak, pitiful man that you've become."

"What's the matter, Mama? You can't stand the sight of your own work?"

"Don't blame you on me. I tried to raise you the right way. You were too busy chasing around that little whorish girl to ever see that."

"Don't you call her a whore. Don't even speak of her. I can't believe I've allowed you to make me hurt so many people that I love. Not anymore. I failed Alieza, but it's not too late for me to save Rumor."

"What are you babbling about?" Lula Mae asked.

"You know damn well what I'm talking about. I'm telling Rumor the truth. I'm telling everybody the truth."

"Get out of here, Bernard. You sicken me."

As Pastor Bernard walked free of the hospice room, he felt a million pounds lighter knowing exactly what he needed to do. Lula Mae screamed with fury, "You think that girl will love you? When she knows the truth, she'll never forgive you. You're no better than me, Bernard. You're my son and you're going to die old and alone just like me." Each of her words resonated in his mind, but at that point, he no longer cared. He raced down the hall thinking only of me.

The automatic sliding doors of the hospital entrance opened, introducing Pastor Bernard to that evening's air. He felt something vibrating in his pocket. He pulled out his cell phone which flashed several missed calls. He immediately returned the calls after seeing they were all from Aunt HoneyBea's house.

"Hello," Cousin Junebug answered.

"Yes, this is Pastor Bernard. Did HoneyBea call me?"

"Oh, yeah. It's the Rev," Cousin Junebug yelled. "She's not here right now. She and Darryl Junior rushed to the hospital with Rumor."

"I'm at the hospital now. Something wrong with Rumor?" Pastor Bernard asked.

"She cut her wrists. She lost a lot of blood. When they left, she was in and out of consciousness. We haven't heard anything else yet." As cousin Junebug spoke, Pastor Bernard felt his head growing lighter by the second.

He dropped his cell phone down onto the pavement. Everything seemed to be spinning. He looked down and closed his eyes hoping to steady himself. A cold hand grabbed his shoulder. He looked up into the decaying eyes of Alieza Arden.

"This is your fault." The vision of Alieza scowled before reaching out to grab his throat.

Rumor's Journal (Entry 9)

Not even the plush, soft wool of the little lamb's hoof
Can hide the daggers in the mouth of the big bad wolf.
Right before my face stood an evil I refused to see
Until that very evil opened wide
and totally consumed me.
Helpless against a predator I chose to believe was prey,
On my knees, to God, I humbly do pray
For the right words that I need to say
In order for all the demons to fade and go away.

Chapter 10

A Brother's Quarrel

It's so funny how we will travel as far as death to find a truth that has been right in front of our faces the entire time. If only we would look beyond the surface lies, but why would we, when the lie seems so much easier to find. This was Hurley's problem. The whole city blindly followed lie after lie. No one questioned anything, because things had always worked perfectly that way. We were all lost in comfort until that one day when the lies no longer worked.

The city council officials stood before a packed building of Hurley's citizens as a majority of hands rose to support Caesar Grimes' new casino initiative. Mayor Clarke stood in the center of the council with beads of sweat dripping from his head. He guzzled down bottles of water to remove the dry, clammy sensation that plagued his mouth. This sensation was not foreign to an alcoholic like Mayor Clarke, but it was the dizzy spells that were alarming him the most. He couldn't figure out why he felt so terrible inside. For the first time since he'd taken the mayoral seat, things were finally going his way. He'd shaken hands with Caesar Grimes and welcomed him back to save their dying city. That day should have been one of internal celebration for him, but his head continued to pound with the increasing pressure of his blood flow.

"Mayor Clarke, are you okay? You're looking kinda sick," Deputy Mayor Sheila Owen whispered into his ear.

"I'm fine, Sheila. Just get me some more water please," Mayor Clarke said just as the city council approved the vote and ended the meeting. Everyone stood to their feet eager to begin that evening's festivities. Many of them headed towards the mayor looking to shake his sweaty palms. Mayor Clarke tried to put his best face forward, but whatever ailed him was clearly not going away.

"Mr. Mayor, you are going to stay and join us for this evening's cookout, right? Mr. Rogers is barbequing and I whipped up a nice batch of my famous lima beans. I know you remember my lima beans. They're the best in the county." Ms. Shirley Evans greeted the mayor while bragging about her horrible lima beans. She was convinced that they were so delicious because no one had the heart to tell her how they really tasted. Local gossip was that animal control used leftover pots of her lima beans to keep rattle snakes out of the city.

"I think I'll be retiring early for the night, Ms. Evans. I've got a lot of paperwork to sign in the morning for this new casino." Mayor Clarke struggled to converse while tugging at his collar to loosen it from around his neck. He was getting hotter with each second.

"You sure about that, Mr. Mayor? You'll be missing out. It's one of my creamiest batches yet. You should see the way those beans just oozed off the tip of the spoon. It's ooey gooey goodness at its best." Ms. Evans continued to ramble on about her lima beans until she noticed that the mayor's cheeks were swelling like two big balloons. "Are you okay, Mr. Mayor? You don't look too hot."

"I'm fine. I just have to go." Mayor Clarke tried to walk around Ms. Evans and dash for the door. With all the talk of those disgusting lima beans, his stomach was upset and he could feel his lunch rising up to his chest.

"Well just take some lima beans with you," Ms. Evans yelled while grabbing the mayor's suit jacket. He turned around fed up with her annoying lima bean offer. In his condition, his patience was short and Sister Evans had just tip toed on his final nerve.

"I don't want any of your revolting lima . . ." Before he could finish his sentence, vomit erupted from his mouth all over Ms. Evans' sundress. She screamed as if she had just seen a ghost. Deputy Mayor quickly rushed out and tossed the bottled water aside as she grabbed the mayor and escorted him through the crowd.

In a far corner of the building, Caesar Grimes stood with a wide grin on his aging face. "Who would've thought? Those herbs of yours worked perfectly. No one will suspect that the drunken fool was poisoned. They'll blame it all on a hangover until he's dead, clearing the way for me to move in and take back my city."

"You just make sure Tuna get what you promise her. Tuna no work for free." Miss Tuna stood to Caesar's right with her arms folded.

"Don't worry, old friend. As this city is about to find out, I always repay my debts." Caesar laughed maniacally before returning his ominous stare to the crowd of unsuspecting people. With a confused look on her face, Miss Tuna followed his gaze out towards Deputy Ron Mack who struggled to control the crowd from the other end of the room.

With Gia so frequently on his mind, Deputy Ron found it hard to concentrate on his job. All he wanted to do was embrace her, kiss her gently and ensure her that everything was going to get better. He hated that he had no idea what was going on in her mind. He was constantly pulling out his cell phone hoping to see that she had returned one of his many phone calls, but she never did.

"Ronald Mack, what's with all this lollygagging, boy? Go on outside and stand watch." Sheriff Mack's words interrupted his son's thoughts.

"My bad, Pops." Just as Ron apologized he saw what looked like Gia walking past him. He didn't get a good look at her face. She was wearing Gia's blazer, and the ring that Gia's mother passed down to her glistened brightly from her dainty little finger. Ron completely ignored his father's order and chased after Gia.

He shouted her name, but she would not stop. Her pace quickened with each step. Before Ron knew it, he was running full speed behind her as she ran out into the woods. They both ran until they could no longer hear the noise of the crowd. It was just the two of them when she finally stopped running. She didn't turn around, but Ron proceeded to talk anyway.

"Gia, I'm sorry for everything. I know you must think I'm a terrible person, but I never wanted any of this to happen. I should've stayed away and let you live a normal life like every other teen aged girl, but I just couldn't shake my feelings for you. I still can't. I know this is wrong with you being so young and then my little brother and all, but I think about you almost every second of the day. When I'm not thinking about you, I'm thinking about the child that we lost and the family that we were supposed to have. I miss you baby, and I don't care if loving you is wrong. That's one wrong that I never want to make right." Tears escaped his eyes as he opened his heart to her.

Slowly she turned around with a full moon shining bright behind her. It almost blurred the sight of her combined with the thick humidity of that night's air. Even with the elements shielding her, it became clear that the girl was not Gia. A gun shot blasted. Birds quickly flew from the surrounding trees causing leaves and branches to fall around them. Ron turned to face the sound of the blasting ammunition. He saw his little brother K Mack standing and gripping a smoking gun barrel, which was pointed towards the sky.

"What the hell is going on here?" Ron shouted.

"Good job, baby." K Mack smiled as the girl rushed to join him by his side.

"Anything for you, boo." She planted a kiss on K Mack's cheek. Now that she faced the moon's light, Ron could finally see her. The girl was Nivea, Sister Emmagene's oldest daughter.

"Finally, big bro. Finally we can get this out of the way. You don't know how long I've been waiting to put a bullet in your backstabbing chest," K Mack said with his finger tightened around the gun's trigger.

"What are you talking about? Don't point that thing at me." Ron stepped forward to take the gun from his brother, but before he could take one full step, K Mack fired a round off at his feet. Ron immediately jumped back to avoid the fire power. "Are you crazy?"

"Don't play stupid, Ron. I know you been smashing Gia, and now so will everybody. I just videotaped that whole sappy ass apology that was meant for my girlfriend. Now when I put this bullet in you, not one jury will convict me for shooting a confessed rapist." K Mack aimed the gun at his brother's head.

"Kendrick, chill out. This is murder that you're talking about here. You can't be serious," Ron pleaded.

"I'm about as serious as a bullet wound. Don't believe me? Just watch. Pow." K Mack grimaced while tightening his finger around the gun's trigger.

Meanwhile at the cookout, Sheriff Mack walked around searching for both his sons. As he scrambled through the citizens of Hurley, he bumped into Sister Emmagene who appeared to be searching for someone as well. She immediately grabbed him with a look of panic in her eyes.

"Sheriff, please tell me that you've seen my daughter, Nivea. I can't find her anywhere. I've got to get out of here. I just got a call from Beatrice that her niece is in the hospital."

"What happened to Rumor?" Sheriff Mack asked.

"How did you know I was talking about Rumor?" the puzzled look on Sister Emmagene's face grew to be even more pronounced.

"Because Gia's here. I saw her a little while ago. My boy went off running in behind her. I've been trying to find both my boys ever since," Sheriff Mack answered.

"Sheriff, that's not possible. We left Gia at home. In fact, she's only been out of that house once since the day of the accident and that was for Alieza's funeral."

"You sure because I could've sworn I saw Gia. She had on that little blazer that she always wears."

"The pretty little blue one?" Sister Emmagene inquired.

"Yeah. That's the one," Sheriff Mack said. As they both stood speechless exchanging confused stares, a gunshot could be heard from deep in the woods.

"Oh my God. What was that?" Sister Emmagene cried.

"Stay here. I'm going to check it out," Sheriff Mack yelled before racing out into the woods.

"Wait. That may be my baby out there," Sister Emmagene screamed before running after him. After the suspected murder of Tavis Tahiri, the city was already on edge. The sound of the gunshots quickly dampened the mood of that evening. Everyone stood frozen facing the forest. They were all afraid of what possibly lay beyond those trees.

"I just love it when a plan comes together." Caesar Grimes maintained a close watch on the events developing throughout the cookout.

"Seems like boy and gal got job done. Tuna knew ring would do trick." Miss Tuna said.

"Yes, I must admit. That was a smart move asking Gia for her mother's ring in exchange for those abortion herbs. With that ring on her finger, there was no way Ron Mack would've ever questioned whether Nivea was Gia or not," Caesar Grimes continued.

"What Caesar promise boy to make him kill him own brother, anyway?" Miss Tuna asked.

"It wasn't hard. K Mack will do anything for the promise of fame. Now with one son dead and another convicted of murder, Sheriff Mack will surely lose his mind," Caesar laughed.

"No mayor, no sheriff, and soon no preacher. The throne of Hurley is primed for Caesar's picking." Miss Tuna smiled with the satisfaction of success.

"Yes, finally a king who deserves to have a queen like myself by his side." First Lady Silvia appeared from behind them.

She scanned the cookout to ensure that no one was looking before quickly caressing Caesar's hand with her own. She looked into his eyes with desire before saying, "Come with me baby. Our throne awaits us."

Deep in the woods, the air was still filled with smoke from the shots blasted by K Mack's gun. K Mack's eyes were locked onto his older brother. He enjoyed the sight of fear as it surged through his brother's veins. He relished the view of Ron's rounded and quivering eye lids. K Mack enjoyed having such power over his older brother. For as long as he could remember, Ron was always better than him. Ron was stronger, faster, and far more intelligent. Ron followed perfectly in their father's footsteps as opposed to K Mack who jumped head first into the thug world of gangster rap. As if it weren't enough that Ron held their father's favor, Ron had also stolen his girlfriend. K Mack was tired of living in Ron's shadow. In his mind, he was the talented one. Despite the fact that no one could see it, he was the better of them, and with his brother finally out of the way, the world would finally be able to accept him as the star that he always knew himself to be.

"Kendrick, don't do this brother. You're angry and I understand why. I was wrong." Ron begged for his brother's forgiveness.

"Oh, but that's one wrong that you never want to make right. Isn't that what you said big bro? Stop begging. It's pathetic," K Mack said.

"Ok, baby. It's kinda' creepy out here. He seems plenty scared to me. Can't we just go back now?" Nivea shivered from within Gia's blazer.

"Shut the hell up, trick," K Mack snapped at Nivea. "This ain't no game. I'm about to murk this fool in real life."

"Wait a minute. You didn't say anything about killing anybody. The plan was to scare him. He's scared. Let's go," Nivea cried.

"Don't be gettin' all cry baby on me, now. We in this together. I go down and you going with me," K Mack smiled.

"Nivea, I don't know how you got yourself into this mess, but it's not too late to turn around. My brother can't make you do anything that you don't want to do." Seeing that she did not want any part of the murder, Ron placed his focus on Nivea.

"Nigga, shut up." K Mack pushed Nivea to the ground and quickly returned the gun's aim to Ron. "I'm done talking. Die slow, big bro."

"K stop." Nivea jumped to her feet and rushed K Mack from behind.

The bullet exploded from the barrel of the gun. Ron closed his eyes tightly to prepare for his death. The sound of the gunfire echoed throughout his ear canal. For a brief second within his mind, everything was quiet. He knew that he was dead until he felt his chest heave outwards with the force of life. Ron opened his eyes to see K Mack on top of Nivea choking the life out of the poor girl. K Mack's anger took control of his mind. He wasn't even aware that his gun lie smoking on the ground beside him. Ron seized the opportunity of the moment and leapt towards the gun. K Mack released Nivea's throat from his grip and reached for the gun as well. Both brothers clasped the weapon into their hands at the same time. Nivea struggled for air as the two brothers fought for the gun. After a few seconds of struggle that seemed more like a few hours, Ron snatched the gun free from K Mack's hands.

"Boys, what's going on back here?" Sheriff Mack rushed onto the scene just as Ron was able to recover the weapon.

"Oh my God. Nivea. What's wrong with my baby?" Sister Emmagene dropped to her knees to tend to her choking daughter.

Then they all watched as a throng of Hurley's citizens gathered from beyond the trees. Everyone froze at the sight of Deputy Ron standing over his baby brother with a gun in his hands. Ron immediately dropped the gun to his side and turned to face his father.

"Ronald Mack, tell me what is going on now," Sheriff Mack demanded.

"Tell him, Ron. Tell him about how you banged my sixteen year old girlfriend and got her pregnant. Tell him brother." K Mack barked while standing to his feet.

"Ron, please tell me that isn't true. Please tell me you haven't been having sex with Gia?" Sheriff Mack asked, but Ron could barely hear him over the whispers of the people. He and Gia's secret was out. Both their lives would never be the same.

"Either you tell him Ron or I'll let the video tell him. Your choice." K Mack continued to hassle his brother.

"I'm sorry, Dad. It's true," Ron confessed. The look of disappointment in his father's eyes was too overwhelming. Ron could no longer look up. The judgment of the people could be felt throughout the woods. There was only one way out of his situation. He took the gun and pressed it against the temporal region of his head.

"Sheriff Mack." The night's breeze carried the screams of a woman from behind the trees.

"Not now. Ron put that gun down now, son." Sheriff Mack tried to ignore the mysterious screams while pleading for his son's life.

"Sheriff Mack." The scream continued as Chrisette Carter appeared from atop a wooded hill. "You and your sons are in danger. You've gotta hear me out before it's too late."

Ron opened his eyes and dropped the gun at the sound of Chrisette's words. All three of the Mack men faced Chrisette with curiosity in their eyes. By the way she panted for air; it was obvious that Chrisette had been urgently rushing to gain their attention.

"I have someone with me who may have some very valuable information about Caesar Grimes," Chrisette said in between deep breathes.

Rumor's Journal (Entry 10)

As I search for death, it haunts my friends
Threatening to see them to the worst possible end
Plaguing their families with the consequences of sin,
How did we find ourselves here once again?
Staring in the eyes of the devil, will our faith bend,
Or will we be strong enough to see our torment end?
In the final hour, we desperately scramble for the win.
Teetering between life and death,
not sure which way to begin.

Chapter 11

HoneyBea's Prayer

I don't know what happened to me in the hours following the slashing of my wrists, but that blade met my arms with a last minute will to live. I remember weeping. Each tear begged for a little more life to live, a few more breathes to breathe and more words to be said; but I felt nothing. Could that have been what death felt like? Was it just a lonely shell of inescapable confusion and regret? It was an overwhelming opportunity to contemplate all of my life's actions. I thought about each and every emotion. My mind even ran across every single person that I was leaving behind. How would they move on without me? How could I have been so selfish? When death took my mother, my world shattered. Ever since that day a giant void existed within me. I was always Alieza's baby. I was always the proud daughter of a saint, a savior, and a true life angel. I was due a natural inheritance to greatness based solely on the fact that my mother dedicated her entire life to those less fortunate. In only one week my entire purpose had become a lie. She was no saint and no amount of prayer could save her. Her entire life was one downhill slope, and as a result, so was mine. Her demise was inevitable, and as my wrists drained dry, so was mine. Now my entire family would fall apart with the news of yet another death. Their shattered fragments would join that same downward slope that would eventually see us all to hell.

Aunt HoneyBea's swollen eyes had not stopped crying once since the ambulance rushed us off into the night. So much guilt weighed heavy on her soul. It was too much even for someone as strong as she was. Darryl Junior joined her in the waiting room. It frightened him to see Aunt HoneyBea so broken down and defeated. Her back was hunched over beneath the weight of grief. Lines of stress ran across the sagging skin of her sulking face. He had no idea the amount of shame that she carried within her conscience. All he could do was watch as she dropped to her knees and called on the only one who could free them from their trials.

> *Father God, creator of heaven and earth, one from whom all life flows, the stars and skies bow to your command, all kings and rulers of this earth yield to kiss your hand. God of light, in You exists no darkness. You are the source of my strength and*

the strength of my life. I lift my hands to You, oh omnipotent, omnipresent, and omniscient God of all beings. I lift my hands in selfless prayer and worship.

Hospital orderlies rushed to the waiting room as Aunt HoneyBea shouted out in prayer. They grabbed her raised arms, "Ma'am, we're going to have to ask you to find a seat and be quiet. You are disturbing others."

"Get your hands off her now." Darryl Junior stood with his fists clenched. He eyed the two orderlies with a threatening stare.

"Sir, please. We're just doing our job here."

"Well so is she, but only her orders are coming from a much higher authority," Darryl Junior explained.

"Either she settles down or we'll be forced to ask you both to leave," the orderly urged.

Aunt HoneyBea continued to pray,

Lord, I humbly stand before you now in need of your everlasting grace and mercy. Lord God I understand that you work in mysterious ways. I know that Your supreme plan for our lives is beyond what my physical mind could ever understand, but I ask as Your child and as Your humble servant that if it is Your will please save my family. Please save them from the wretched mistakes of my past. Lord, I know you warned me about placing others before You. I know that I was not obedient and that I put my own will and desires before Your own. Father, I'm sorry. I'm sorry for not yielding to Your perfect will.

I loved a man and I held him high as an idol within my heart. I sacrificed everything that I believed to keep him. I put him before You, myself, and my family. Lord, I put him before my family. I allowed my love for him to cause me to turn my back on my baby sister when she needed me most. She cried to me for help. She told me that he touched her. He invaded her innocence. I was supposed to protect her innocence. I was supposed to shield her from evil and guide her in Your light. But through my own flesh, all I saw was darkness. I chose to believe his lies even when her truth was so obvious. I was so angry with her truth. I was so angry with her that I allowed the world to destroy her. I watched as the evils of this world destroyed my baby sister and I did nothing. Lord please forgive me. Please forgive my family. My sister is gone, but the best of her still lives. She gifted us with the most beautiful soul this world has ever seen. She gave us Rumor. Lord, You gave us Rumor;

and if it is Your will, allow us to keep her.
Allow me to protect her innocence. Allow
me to right the wrongs that, through my
disobedience, I unleashed onto my family.

Darryl Junior stood in awe of our aunt's confessions. He had no idea that Tony P was capable of such evil. He had always held the man in such high regard. Tony P was the primary influence for his alter ego, DJ the Spade. In a game of cards, the spade is a strong suite, but there's not one heart among them. Darryl Junior's eyes were finally opened. For the first time, he saw the monster that he had become. He had allowed the heartless spade to hurt Chrisette. It was no wonder she had left him. No woman could love a man modeled after such a heartless monster like Tony P.

Aunt HoneyBea continued,

Please, Jesus. Please, help me. I opened my
home to Satan and I gave him my heart. I
cursed my own home and everyone within
it. It's not their fault, Lord. They shouldn't
have to pay for the lies that I've told to
myself. I'm tired of lying God. I'm tired of
disobeying Your will. Please tell me what
to do. Tell me how to fix this. Tell me how
to save my family. Tell me how to save
Rumor.

Aunt HoneyBea's prayer unleashed a presence that could be felt throughout that entire hospital. Her words were so powerful that even the orderlies started to weep. The other patrons of the waiting room cried out for God as well. They cried out for Hurley's redemption. As worship and praise rung throughout the hospital, Darryl Junior looked down at his cell phone. The name across the screen was definitely evidence of God's presence. It was Chrissy.

"Hello, Chrissy, is that you?" Darryl Junior answered.

"Oh my God, Darryl. Thank God, you're okay. Come down to the Sheriff's office now. There are some things that you need to know." He could hear fear in the shaking of her voice.

"Chrissy, I'm at the hospital. Rumor's hurt herself."

"Okay, stay there. I'll tell the Sheriff. We're coming to you," Chrissy said before ending the phone call.

Darryl Junior was left in frightening suspense after the phone call. The tone in Chrissy's voice expressed a level of fear and vulnerability that he'd never heard from her before. He couldn't imagine what could be so wrong that it would cause the sheriff to come see him. The nervous energy developing within him was a sharp contrast to the praise and excitement that was around him. He glanced over at Aunt HoneyBea as she kneeled in the middle of the waiting room with her hands stretched towards the ceiling. Seeing our aunt so vulnerable was even more alarming than the softness he'd heard from

Chrissy. Aunt HoneyBea was always the one who held the family together. That's when the root of all their pain became so clear to him. Alieza was at the center of it all.

Darryl Junior didn't know the true story of exactly why Alieza had left all those years ago. He was too young to understand any of it, but somehow he always knew that none of their stories made sense. He'd seen Alieza with me. He'd seen the way she looked at me and cared for me above all else. From day one, she was so protective of me, never wanting to let me out of her sight. He'd witnessed Alieza's love for me, so the abandonment never made sense to him. Darryl Junior then thought back to the night he found Alieza. He contemplated on his negotiations with Caesar Grimes for his aunt's life.

Caesar smiled with the most conniving grin as they finally agreed on the terms of their negotiations. Darryl Junior would surrender his shares of Gulf Gamble and Caesar would release Alieza to Darryl's care. It seemed to be a simple and reasonable trade at the time. Alieza was his family. Who wouldn't forfeit stock for their own family? In that moment, he imagined that he'd be the hero. He could see the smile on my face when he would bring Alieza back to me. He could see us all gathered around a table full of Aunt HoneyBea's best foods. We would all laugh and fellowship as if nothing had ever come between us. It was the happy ending that influenced Darryl Junior's decision, but there had not been one happy moment since that day.

Hurley was the perfect habitat for lies and Alieza was like one big bomb of truth. Darryl Junior's eyes widened as he realized the true reason that she had left. Alieza knew all too well the potential pain that the truth would cause. She left and stayed away to protect someone from the truth. She was protecting someone who she cared about more than anything else in this world. She was protecting . . ."Rumor."

"Aunt HoneyBea. Aunt HoneyBea," Darryl Junior yelled.

"Lord, please give me the strength to be the firm foundation that my family needs. Lord please be with me. Please . . ." Aunt HoneyBea continued to pray and weep.

"Auntie, listen to me." Darryl Junior grabbed both of Aunt HoneyBea's hands and looked into her weeping eyes. "I can't explain it but something is seriously wrong. We need to go see Rumor now. I have a feeling that she's in danger."

"Baby, the doctor's won't let us see her yet. We just have to believe in God that she'll come out of this," Aunt HoneyBea said.

"No, Auntie, you're not listening to me. Chrissy just called me and something is wrong. And for some reason, Caesar Grimes' creepy smile keeps flashing in my head."

"Caesar Grimes? Darryl, how do you know that wicked man?"

"He's an old pimp down in Biloxi. I didn't want to tell you this, but Alieza was hooking for him."

"I'd heard gossip that that man had returned, but I didn't think they were true. If Caesar Grimes is somehow involved in any of this, then there is trouble coming." Aunt HoneyBea stood while staring off into empty space.

"Yeah, Caesar's back. He spoke at the Town Hall meeting a couple of hours ago. He's building a casino over there where Nelson Paper is shutting down." A coughing woman stood after hearing Aunt HoneyBea mention Caesar's name.

"Caesar Grimes was at the town hall? Why?" Aunt HoneyBea asked.

"HoneyBea, we were all surprised but I think the man has changed. I even spotted him having a nice, long conversation in the corner with First Lady Silvia. They seemed awfully close, almost like they'd known each other for years," the lady explained.

"Yeah. He almost killed her husband and vowed to one day finish the job," Aunt HoneyBea said.

"Something is not right, Auntie. What are we going to do?" Darryl Junior inquired.

Aunt HoneyBea stomped over to the receptionist desk and demanded, "Get a doctor now. I need to see my niece."

"Ma'am just calm down and have a seat. We'll page a doctor momentarily," the receptionist said.

"Sweety, I said now." Aunt HoneyBea slammed her purse down on the desk. She gave that receptionist a stare of intimidation that only Aunt HoneyBea could muster. Everyone in Hurley knew that look on Aunt

HoneyBea's face. It was a clear sign that she meant business. The receptionist quickly picked up the phone and paged a doctor.

Moments later Aunt HoneyBea and Darryl Junior were being ushered into the intensive care to find me. The nurses walked them into my room, but I was not there.

"Where is she? Where is my baby?" Aunt HoneyBea screamed.

"Ma'am, we can assure you that she was here a few moments ago," one of the nurses gasped.

"What do you mean you can assure me? Where is Rumor?" Aunt HoneyBea screamed while launching towards the nurse. Darryl Junior seized Aunt HoneyBea just as she was seconds away from grabbing the nurse's throat.

"HoneyBea. Darryl Junior." Sheriff Mack's voice and the tapping of his boots could be heard as he followed the sound of Aunt HoneyBea's scream into the intensive care unit.

"Auntie, it's the sheriff," Darryl Junior grunted while struggling to hold back our aunt.

"Good, tell him he'd better get ready to book me because I'm gon' strangle one of these heifers," Aunt HoneyBea exclaimed.

"Ma'am, please calm down, this is the ICU for God's sake." One of the nurses pleaded with Aunt HoneyBea.

"Then honey, you are in the right place for what I'm about to unleash on you." Aunt HoneyBea continued to reach for the women.

"HoneyBea, calm down," Sheriff Mack said in between deep breathes of exhaustion caused by his race through the hospital hallways.

"Sheriff, Chrissy said you had something to tell me," Darryl Junior said.

"I'll do you one better, son. We've got someone I'm sure you would love to talk to." As Sheriff Mack spoke, Deputy Ron stepped into view. There was a man in front of him, who was bound by handcuffs. The man's head hung low so that Darryl Junior could not see his face.

"What's going on here, Sheriff?" Darryl Junior nervously asked.

"Show your face, punk," Sheriff Mack said. The man swung his head upwards into the light revealing himself to be Darryl Junior's best friend, Red.

"I'm sorry, DJ. I got greedy, man. I didn't want anybody to get hurt," Red whimpered apologetically.

"Red, what have you done?" Darryl Junior said.

"He's going to tell you everything, but first is Rumor okay?" Sheriff Mack asked.

"No, she's gone. Somebody say something. Where is my baby?" Aunt HoneyBea cried.

"I'm sorry, man." Red's eyes filled with tears.

"What have you done? Where is Rumor?" Darryl Junior yelled while attempting to attack Red.

Sheriff Mack firmly placed his hand on Darryl Junior's shoulder, both stopping him and slightly calming him. "Okay, son, it's time to talk or I'm going to let Darryl Junior here beat the dog doo doo out of your punk ass."

"If she's gone, 9 out of 10 times, Caesar has her. I didn't know exactly what he was up to, DJ. You have to believe me. He just started asking me all these questions about you, where you were from, and your family. I helped him get to you by hiring Alieza for Funyun. I thought, what was the worst that could happen. I just wanted some of that Gulf Gamble stock for myself. You have to believe that I didn't mean for anyone to get hurt," Red answered while again dropping his head in shame.

"You asshole. I should've known I couldn't trust you. What would he want with Rumor? It doesn't make any sense," Darryl Junior asked.

"He said something about the Reverend's lies caused him to lose his daughter, and now he's evening the score," Red explained.

"His daughter? Who is his daughter?" Darryl Junior questioned.

"I can answer that part, son. Louise Vazquez is Caesar Grimes' only child. When he was tried for the attempted murder of Bernard Johnson, his entire drug dealing operations were exposed. Caesar did 5 years before he was paroled. After that, Louise had Taylor and she didn't want her new family to have anything to do with her drug dealing father. She took Manny's last name and Caesar was officially dead to her," Sheriff Mack said further clarifying the situation.

"Where does Rumor fit into any of this?" Darryl said.

"Oh God. I hoped to never have to speak on this. God forgive us all, Rumor is Pastor Bernard's daughter." Aunt HoneyBea's eyes filled with shame as the confession left her lips.

Rumor's Journal (Entry 11)

They say where is Rumor?
Search left, search right, ain't seen her later nor sooner.
Somewhere over the horizon beneath the lunar,
Eclipsed from the world by those
who seek to doom her.
But somehow even I don't know where I am.
Been knowing them all my life
and I can't even trust my fam.
I heard my auntie's prayer and I said no ma'am.
How can I even begin to forgive when your lies done
left me damned?

Chapter 12

A Father's Way

Sometimes our memories deceive us. We remember what brings us the most comfort, but we reject those memories that bring pain. Although this seems to be the perfect coping mechanism, it isn't. The pain is important. We need to remember the pain because it's the only thing we have that reminds us to never allow the hurt again.

When I was a small child, I remember my mother taking me to a place. It was a beautiful place. A stone white gazebo with pillars shaped like arch angels stood erect in the center of a glamorous garden. Some of the greenest grass I've ever laid eyes on extended into the purest pastures. Flowered bushes lined a trail that led through the center of the pasture directly into the middle of the gazebo. A string of ponies galloped up and down the pastures like fanciful, little children. The sun was at its brightest on that day. As usual, its rays seemed to follow my mother like her own personal spotlight. Together we jumped aboard the back of an almond-colored pony. She and I, mother and daughter, rode across the garden like ships on a sea of greenery.

There was only perfection in those memories. They were among the best that I had, but just like in the perfect Garden of Eden, somehow the serpent still squirmed among us. Fast forward many years when my mother's body was freshly buried and she existed only as that memory, I lay asleep directly in the center of the same stone white gazebo. If it had not been so beautiful, it would have been frightening. It looked exactly as I remembered it.

"If the truth's gonna hurt, then I gotta tell a lie . . ." A man's voice sung the lyrics to my mother's song. He had the perfect tempo and tone. It was as if she was singing through him. I looked up to see Pastor Bernard's smiling face.

"Pastor? Where are we?" I asked.

"Call me Lucky. There are things that I've done in my past that made me hate that name, but standing here looking into your eyes, the name's never felt more appropriate," he said while standing in front of the sunlight.

"So you are Lucky? You're the man from my mother's mural too, aren't you? What's going on Pastor?" I continued to ask.

"Your mother's mural? How do you know about the mural?"

"That's right, I'm not supposed to know, am I? I'm not supposed to know anything. You hid it beneath the church just like the church hid her beneath the ground. I don't know much about my mother, but I hate you all for what you did to her," I said.

"Rumor, it's not what you think. I'm going to tell you everything," Lucky said while sitting beside me on the bench inside the gazebo.

"I don't want any more lies. Stay away from me," I screamed. Looking at him, I didn't see the man who I'd always known as Pastor Bernard. I saw the shadow man from my mother's mural. He was Lucky, the man who had somehow hurt my mother and destroyed the purity that was left within her.

"Please, listen to me," Lucky yelled as I swung my fists to fight him away.

"No more lies," I screamed as tears streamed down my face.

"Please Rumor, you're going to hurt your wrists again. Just allow me to finally tell you the truth, and if after hearing everything you still want nothing to do with me, then I will leave you alone. I promise."

I calmed myself and held my wrist close to my body because the pain of the quarrel was too much for my wounds. I looked up into his eyes and searched for signs of sincerity. I had been told so many lies. How could I trust him to tell me the truth? That's when I saw her. I'm not sure if it was a trick of my eyes or just a wishful sight, but she materialized within the light of the sun. My mother stood by his side and placed her hand on his shoulder. She nodded to me as if she could hear my wondering mind. She nodded to give him her approval. Then she smiled. It would be the last time that I'd ever see that beautiful smile outside of a portrait or a memory. She smiled wide and blew me a kiss before vanishing into the Sunday morning light.

"Okay. Tell me everything," I said to Lucky.

It was exactly nine months before the day of my birth, Lucky remembered sleeping soundly. A thunderstorm raged outside of his home. The branch of a nearby tree repeatedly slammed against his window. Even in his sleep, he could hear the knocking of the branch, but suddenly the knocking was accompanied by her familiar voice. As if her voice were magic, even the quietest whisper instantly reached him from the deepest depths of his slumber.

"Lucky," Alieza whispered.

"Lieza, what are you doing out there in the rain?" Lucky squinted through tired eyes to take in the sight of her wet hair clinging to her drenched brown skin.

"I needed to see you. Please meet me at the gazebo."

"Lieza, it's gotta be past midnight. You know if my mother catches you here, she'll kill us both."

"Please, meet me at the gazebo," she said before jumping down into the wet grassy grounds beneath his window.

Thunder struck just as her feet met the ground. The loud banging of the dark skies sent a feeling of fear through Lucky that reminded him of his mother. He thought of the sharp blade that she'd pressed tightly against his throat. He knew that she'd meant business. He knew that she'd kill him if he ever brought shame to the family name by being caught with Alieza, but he could not deny his heart. He loved Alieza and his heart wouldn't allow him to pass up even one moment with her.

Lucky wrapped himself in a robe and rushed out into the stormy night. Lucky's parents owned a large, secluded plantation home just outside of Hurley. In the backyard, there was a giant beautiful garden that surrounded a stone white gazebo. He met Alieza at the gazebo.

She was soaking wet, but from the look of her swollen eyes, it was not just because of the rain. She had been crying. Lucky enveloped her tiny frame with his broad arms. He held her closely as she proceeded to sob onto his shoulder. He could feel her body trembling. Her body's vibrations were not the result of the cold and windy rainstorm. She was afraid. She was hurt. He'd come to know Alieza better than anyone, and he could feel that something was terribly wrong.

"Alieza, what's going on?" Lucky asked while looking deep into her eyes. Even in her drenched and distraught state, her eyes were still like the kindest mirrors. Having been raised by a woman who constantly berated him, Lucky's self-image was dangerously low, but through the eyes of Alieza he loved the man who looked back.

"I can't go home, Lucky. I need your help. Please." She cried before pulling Lucky back into her embrace.

"But Lieza . . ." He feared the consequences of taking her into his home where his hateful mother slept, but even more so he feared the thought of abandoning her with her pain. To Lucky, Alieza was the only light in a world full of shadows. She was every color of the spectrum directly in the midst of a black and white film.

"Please." Alieza pleaded.

"Ok. Follow me." He couldn't deny her but he also feared the wrath of his mother, Lula Mae. There was one place that he knew his mother would never find them. It was also the one place that he feared the most. Beneath their large plantation-styled mansion, there was a dark, creepy basement. It was the same basement that Lula Mae had used so many times before to torture and punish Lucky. Just the thought of being there, disturbed him to the core of his soul. With Alieza trembling within his arms, none of that seemed to matter. He had to protect her. If his prison was her only salvation, then he was willing to spend a lifetime in bondage just for a moment of her happiness.

There was a secret door in the back of their home which lead down into the basement. It was hidden beneath the flower bushes that surrounded the house. Lucky's father had told him that the entrance was once used by run-away slaves. The basement beneath their home was a popular spot on the Underground Railroad. Many slaves had found solace in the cold, dirty tunnel that traced a path from the doorway to the basement. Many of them, either exhausted or injured by the dangers of their escape, died within the confines of the basement. During many nights Lucky could hear the howling of their spirits echoing their cries for freedom. Many of the souls were angry as they never made it beyond the dark, wretched under-belly of Mississippi. Many of them sought vengeance. The living served as their victims. Locked within the basement, Lucky was often their favorite victim.

"Lucky, you don't have to do this," Alieza whispered as they stood atop the stairwell which led down into the dark basement tunnel. "I know what you've been through down there. I don't want you to have to relive it."

"Yeah, but I was only a boy then. I'm a man now and I have to get you out of this rain." Lucky put on a brave face for Alieza, but deep down he knew that the fear still existed within him. He took one large gulp attempting to swallow all of his anxiety and reservations before taking the first step into the basement.

Just as his feet touched the wooden step, thunder rocked the ground beneath them. The sky lit up with a frightening amount of intensity. The lightening illuminated the dark path down the steps. Lucky stood frozen in time as the souls of the dead slaves reached towards him. His heart raced within his chest. His mind was lost to frenzy as their howls consumed his thoughts.

"Lucky, are you okay?" Alieza watched from behind as the wooden stairs rattled beneath the trembling of Lucky's nerves.

"I'm fine." Lucky lied. He looked backwards into Alieza's eyes. Through them, he could see the reflection of the stairway beneath him, but through her eyes, there were no ghosts. He found courage in her presence. The courage was just enough for him to take the next step. He held her hand tightly as she walked behind him. He could feel her pulse through her wrists. With the rhythm of her heart guiding him, he continued to descend into the basement.

Minutes later, they stepped down onto the dirty floors of the basement tunnel. The spirits around him grew even more irate. He could hear his mother's voice lecturing him as the ghosts screamed and scratched against the walls. Lula Mae yelled, "You are a disgrace to this family. I am ashamed to call you my son. I'll lock you in that basement and let you die before I allow you to defame your father's name."

"No. No. Shut up," Lucky hollered through clenched teeth.

"Lucky, it's ok. There's nobody here, but us. It's just me and you. No one's going to hurt you," Alieza said.

"Don't you hear her? She's going to kill us both, Lieza. We have to get out of here." Lucky could no longer maintain his facade of strength. Lula Mae was in his mind. The combination of her threats and the spirits surrounding him was too much for him to bear.

"Just close your eyes, Lucky. Listen to my voice. It's just you and I," Alieza said before humming a song.

"You came and gave the best part of me. Just your heartbeat was my every dream." The words played out within Lucky's mind as Alieza's humming calmed him. Suddenly he could no longer hear the screams of the dead slaves or the nagging of his mother's voice. There was only Alieza and he found strength within her beauty. He opened his eyes and together, they continued to walk to the basement.

The basement was huge, but there was so much clutter that it seemed to be only inches small. There were large boxes filled with all sorts of knick knacks. Hideous African masks decorated the walls. The unbearable stench of neglect flowed from every corner. He and Alieza sat before a bookshelf that was planted sturdily against the wall. Its shelves were lined with all sorts of classics. Alieza loved to read and under any other circumstances, this would have been her dream situation. She rubbed her hand across the dusty spines of the books, taking in each of their titles with her eyes. For the first time that night, she smiled. Lucky's mouth formed into a smile as well while he watched her eyes grow brighter.

Alieza could feel his stare calling her name, so she turned to face him. "Lucky, this is amazing. I've never seen so many books outside of a library."

"If you think that's amazing, you're going to love this." Lucky stood to his feet and pulled her up after him. Ordinarily he was too frightened to explore the contents of the basement, but with Alieza as his company he feared nothing. He darted to the center of the floor and shoved a few boxes to the side, uncovering an old dirty merry-go-round.

"Oh my God!" Alieza gasped.

"It was mine when I was younger. My dad bought if for my fifth birthday. I remember playing on this thing every day."

"Does it work?" Alieza asked.

"I don't know. We're about to find out as soon as I find an outlet for this plug." Lucky pushed the plug into the wall and within moments, the old Merry-Go-Round illuminated with beautiful light and hypnotic sound.

"It's so beautiful." Alieza beamed. "But won't your mother hear us."

"The basement is sound proof. It was used to hide slaves on the Underground Railroad many years ago. There are layers of cement between these walls. She can't hear anything," Lucky explained before jumping onto the Merry-Go-Round as it spun in circles.

"You are crazy," Alieza giggled.

"Only about you." Lucky smiled while reaching his arm out for her to grab on. Alieza took his arm and hopped onto the Merry-Go-Round as well. They leaned against the handles while facing one another. Alieza sung along with the music. Her voice was sweet and pure with a vocal texture that was as smooth as honey. Her hair flew with the slight wind force generated by the spinning toy. They both smiled and laughed while never once removing their gaze from one another's eyes.

"Lucky, I could stay down here with you forever," Alieza said.

"No, this place isn't fit for an angel. There's a whole world out there for us, Alieza. Let's run away. Me and you. Let's run away from our problems together."

"I don't know, Lucky. Mama always said the past has a way of catching up to you."

"With all due respect to your mama's memory Alieza, she never had a chance to see me run. I went All-State on the track team two years in a row. I don't know of any past that could ever catch me."

Alieza smiled at Lucky's humor, but her thoughts of her recent past quickly caught up with her. She dropped her head with sorrow before jumping off the Merry-Go-Round. Lucky unplugged the toy and then walked off after her.

"Alieza what happened to you today?" he asked while grabbing her hand.

"I'm ashamed." She cried.

"Ashamed of what? C'mon. You know that you can tell me anything."

"My innocence is gone. He stole it. I don't know what to do, Lucky." Alieza wept wildly.

"Who?"

"Tony P came home drunk as usual. He always looks at me with that creepy stare, but today was different. It was worse. I was in my nighty. I had been asleep. I only came out for a quick glass of milk but I should not have come out in my nighty. HoneyBea always gets on me about walking around the house in my nighty. It's all my fault. Your mother's right about me. I'm a whore."

"No. She's not right, and Tony P is going to pay for this. I'll make sure of it. You didn't deserve to be hurt that way, Lieza. Nothing you could have done would have made it okay for him to rape you."

"You can't say anything about this. Please."

"I'm not going to be quiet on this. He hurt you. He has to pay."

"HoneyBea will hate me. She told me to stop walking around the house in my nighty. She told me that ladies should be covered up in the company of gentlemen. I should've listened. Please, Lucky. Please promise me that you won't say anything."

"But Lieza . . ." Lucky interjected.

"I said please," Alieza demanded.

"Fine, but you're not going back there tonight. You're staying here with me."

"Wait. What? Tony P raped my mother?" I couldn't digest anymore of the story. My mind was puzzled. Was Tony P my father? I dared not ask him. It was 9 months before my birth. Of course, Tony P was my father. I couldn't breathe. I was the child of a rapist. I was the product of incest. It wasn't blood incest, but incest none the less. In that moment, I couldn't imagine anything worse.

"Yeah. Things were never the same with her and HoneyBea after that day. Your mother feared Tony P and she felt shamed before HoneyBea. At least she said it was shame. On some level, I think she resented your aunt for not protecting her. My mom eventually found the two of us together that night. She beat me within an inch of my life. I made Alieza hide behind the boxes. She eventually returned home, but she couldn't stand being around Tony P. She hated him and she wanted him dead. The only thing that could've prevented her from taking his life was her own innocence. He'd already taken that from her. Tony P was diagnosed with cancer. His medicine was the only thing maintaining him. Your mother secretly switched his prescription pills with some over the counter drug. Within a month, Tony P had died. His autopsy showed no signs of the cancer medication in his body. The guilt overcame your mother and she confessed to HoneyBea. All hell broke loose. HoneyBea hated her. My mother had already labeled Alieza as an outcast and turned the entire church against her. Without HoneyBea, she crumbled beneath the pressure. You were only a child. She didn't want you to be raised around so much hatred, but she couldn't afford to take care of you on her own."

"So she left me?" I asked.

Lucky only looked at me and nodded. "But she didn't leave you alone. That's what I want to tell you Rumor. She left you with your . . ."

"Shut up." I screamed. I was possessed by so much anger, shame and confusion. I didn't know what to think anymore. My father was a rapist and my mother was his murderer. As their child, I could only have been a monster. I didn't want to hear anymore. I'd had enough of the story.

"Rumor, please, let me finish."

"Finish what? I'm the child of a rapist and my mother left me to rot in her shame. I don't want to hear anymore."

"Rumor, no. You're not . . ."

"Shut up . . ." I screamed again before running away. I dashed through the high grass of the yard towards the large house.

"Rumor, wait!" I could hear Lucky yell before the sound of a gunshot blasted through the air. Above me, birds dispersed. I looked back to see Pastor Bernard with a blood stain spreading across the front of his shirt. I didn't see Lucky anymore. Lucky was supposed to be the man from the mural. Lucky was supposed to be the missing piece in the puzzle that was my life, but Lucky was none of the above. Tony P was my father. Lucky was Pastor Bernard, and Pastor Bernard was dying from a gunshot to his chest.

"Run. Run little girl. He can't protect you now." Lucky fell face first into the grass and Caesar Grimes stood tall from behind him holding a smoking gun in hand. I turned around and raced towards the house.

Caesar knelt down beside Pastor Bernard and flipped his body over to face him. First Lady Silvia and Miss Tuna walked into view over Caesar's left and right shoulders. Pastor Bernard took one look at First Lady Silvia and coughed out a pool of blood as he attempted to question why.

"You are so pathetic, Pastor, or should I say Un-Lucky." Caesar laughed. "This is simply revenge. Try not to take it too personally. You and that lying mother of yours ruined my life. I've done some terrible things in my past, but what's so ironic to me is that I went to prison for the one thing that I didn't do. You and your mother left my daughter fatherless. I never beat you. I never even laid a hand on you until today."

Pastor Bernard closed his eyes and prepared for death. He was convinced that it was a death he deserved. Caesar was right. The rumors were all lies. Caesar Grimes had never beaten Lucky for hurting Louise. Lucky was almost beaten to death by his own mother, Lula Mae. Lula Mae had found him and Alieza that night in the basement. She had found them as they both comforted the other with a night of unforgettable passion. Neither of them could hear her as she slowly crept into the basement, because they were locked in the thralls of love-making. Alieza needed Lucky's touch to erase the fowl handprints Tony P had left on her body. She needed him to erase the pain, and Lucky needed Alieza to cool the demons that danced within his own mind. As they made love, they both found freedom, but it was a short found freedom as Lula Mae slammed a bat against her son's unsuspecting head.

"Yeah, close your eyes, weak little boy. Close your eyes and die while I savor in vengeance. You took my daughter from me, so now I'm about to go in that house and kill yours," Caesar gloated.

Pastor Bernard was close to death. He had completely given up on life until Caesar reminded him of the only one who mattered. By threatening to kill me, his only child, Caesar provided him the strength that he needed to continue breathing. Caesar, Silvia and Miss Tuna entered the house searching for me. They all assumed that Pastor Bernard had met death, but he struggled to breathe with thoughts of me.

Me, on the other hand, I remember beating against the doors of the house. They were all locked. I was sure that I was going to die. No one would even hear me scream as far as we were from town. Caesar was going to kill me and there was nowhere for me to hide. I took a deep breath and then I thought of Pastor Bernard's story. I thought of the secret door beneath the bushes.

I scrambled around the house, shuffling through every inch of those bushes until I found the doorway. Quickly I opened the door and ignored the overwhelming must that permeated from within. I dashed down the steps into the darkness of my mother's own history.

Rumor's Journal (Entry 12)

Down the trail of doom,
the pain of the past shall surface again.
It is the greatest known sin,
anti-redemption for gentleman,
To lie upon the truth of the innocent,
leaving them filthy, scarred, and afraid.
It is a loan made in blood,
an agreement that will not go unpaid.
Now it is time for all tables to turn, they'll dance in
circles while a new day has begun.
Bless the child in the midst of the confusion,
because to my being this has been a fatal intrusion.

Chapter 13

Break the Snake

Sheriff Mack and Darryl Junior assembled a search party and swept through Hurley in search of me. No stone was left unturned as they made their way through every street of the city. Aunt HoneyBea stayed behind at the hospital. She was weakened with guilt. She couldn't help but blame herself for everything that had transpired. Every second that passed with no call from Darryl Junior left her even more stressed than the one before it. As the matriarch of our family, Aunt HoneyBea had prided herself on always being in control, but in this situation, she felt totally helpless.

"Beatrice, here's some coffee, hun. You look like you haven't slept in days." Sister Emmagene sat down beside Aunt HoneyBea with a piping hot cup of coffee.

"It's Honey . . . oh never mind." Aunt HoneyBea sighed deeply.

"I'm sorry darling. This is entirely my fault. If I had just stayed away from you and your family, none of this would've happened. I had no idea my daughter was involved in this kind of mess. I just wish there was something that I could do. I hate seeing you so down. I mean I know that you don't like me much. I was kinda' hoping that I could change your mind about me. All I wanted was for us to be friends. You're such a strong woman. I've always envied that about you. I wish I were even half as strong as you. God, why can't I handle my daughters the way you do your girls? This is my fault. I'm so sorry, Beatrice." Sister Emmagene burst into tears.

"Emmagene, quit all that crying. You're going to get tears in my coffee, girl," Aunt HoneyBea said while grabbing the coffee cup from Sister Emmagene's fingers. "I appreciate the kind words, but my family was messed up long before you and your girls came along. I'm not as strong as you think I am. I failed my family."

"With all due respect Beatrice, that's not the way that I see it. You are raising two of your sister's kids on your own. Gia's got your strength and confidence. You should hear how my Nivea would brag about Gia. I swear she would give her last drop of blood just to be your niece. I know what she did to Gia is unforgivable, but I also know that it came from a place of pure admiration. And then there's Rumor. There's a light in that little girl's eyes unlike anything that I've ever seen before. She's so smart, HoneyBea. I mean just from listening to her, I'd swear she had the soul of a woman twice her age. She's got your wisdom. Everyone adores that sweet lil thing. You did a great job raising someone else's children, a much better job than I have done with my own girls," Sister Emmagene continued.

"They do have strength and wisdom, but it didn't come from me. My mama died when Alieza was only a little girl. I was barely an adult myself, and all of a sudden I had to be my sister's mother. I didn't know what I was doing. I was so scared of doing it on my own. I needed help. And that's when he came along. The answer to all my prayers. He was a suave, smoothe talker with gambling skills to pay the bills. I fell in love. I fell hard, honey. That man was all I could think about. I thought about him so much that I forgot the one responsibility that my mama left me. All she wanted me to do was take care of my baby sister. I failed. I chose to believe a drunken fool over my own blood. When she told me that he raped her, deep down I knew that it was true. I just didn't wanna believe her. I didn't wanna be alone. He was everything to me, and when he died I felt alone. Instead of turning to my sister for comfort, I rejected her. I threw her to the wolves just like I had by leaving her alone with that monster Tony P."

"Beatrice, there was no way that you could've known. It's not your fault."

"It is my fault. I abandoned my sister when she needed me most. My mama told me to take care of her and I didn't. Then Alieza told me to take care of Rumor and I haven't, but that's about to change." Aunt

HoneyBea stood from the hospital bench and stared off into the distance.

"What are you going to do?" Sister Emmagene asked.

"Exactly what I should've done a long time ago . . ." Aunt HoneyBea darted down the hallway with a new found sense of fervor. Sister Emmagene stood and ran after her.

Unsure of Aunt HoneyBea's mindset and afraid of what she might be planning to do; Sister Emmagene refused to even blink as she was afraid to let my aunt out of her sights. She watched with confusion as they made their way into the hospital's hospice unit. Aunt HoneyBea finally stopped a few steps short of a door. She stood silently contemplating while facing the name on the door before her. It read, Lula Mae Johnson.

"Oh my God. First Lady Lula Mae? I always assumed that woman was dead. How long has she been here?" Sister Emmagene gasped at the sight of the name plate. Before Sister Emmagene could fully collect her thoughts, Aunt HoneyBea pushed her way into Lula Mae's room.

Aunt HoneyBea stepped slowly as she took in the sight of the frail and sickly old woman panting into the hospital's breathing tube. Lula Mae was a mere shadow of the woman she used to be. Aunt HoneyBea always admired the image of First Lady Lula Mae as she stood strong and bold like an undefeated spiritual warrior. In her prime years, Lula Mae was both respected and feared throughout Hurley, but lying in the hospice bed, she existed merely as an object to be pitied.

"Why are we in here?" Sister Emmagene whispered so as not to awaken Lula Mae.

"Because HoneyBea wants answers. Long time, no see young lady." Lula Mae spoke with a weak, raspy voice. Sister Emmagene's eyes bucked widely as if she were seeing a ghost, but Aunt HoneyBea's look of pity quickly transitioned to one of utter contempt.

"Lula Mae. Still breathing, I see. I guess it's true what they say. Evil never dies," Aunt HoneyBea quipped.

"Oh my God. I think I need to have a seat," Sister Emmagene said as the tension grew to be overwhelming within the room.

"HoneyBea, you always were a tough cookie. It's such a shame that you came from a family of harlots. You really could've been somebody." Lula Mae spoke in between loud, dry coughs.

"You old dried up prune, don't you ever speak on my family. You hear me, you witch. Don't you ever speak on my family," Aunt HoneyBea demanded.

"Calm down, HoneyBea. What are you going to do, kill a dying woman? Go ahead. Be my guest. Unleash me from my suffering," Lula Mae said.

"I wouldn't dare do you any favors," Aunt HoneyBea retorted.

"Then get on with it. Why are you here? What do you want to know from me?" Lula Mae asked.

"I couldn't believe how all of these terrible things were happening to my family over such a short period of time. For a while, I even believed that God was somehow punishing me, but then I thought . . ." Aunt HoneyBea said.

"What did you think?" Lula Mae questioned.

"That the serpent was more subtle than any beast of the field which the Lord God had made," Aunt HoneyBea said quoting the book of Genesis. "This mess has your stench all over it, Lula Mae. I've allowed you to bring shame down on my family for far too long."

"What are you trying to insinuate, young lady?" Lula Mae snapped.

"Insinuate? Nah, see I'm coming out and saying it. You're an evil, old woman who bullied my poor mother into the grave. Then when you no longer had her to bully, you took it out on my baby sister. You disgust me. Where is my niece?"

"Ladies, I do not understand this. We're all church family. What is it with all the animosity?" Sister Emmagene asked.

"I'll tell you where it's coming from, Emmagene. She's a jealous fool who has always envied my family. Her mother was nothing more than a maid who wiped the dust from my floors. The poor girl wanted my life so badly that she coveted my husband. Then her whore of a daughter seduced my son. Your family is a cancer to this town. Too bad I couldn't muster up enough radiation to wipe you all out," Lula Mae said before bursting into an intense coughing fit.

"Now you hold up, Mrs. Lula Mae, Beatrice is one of the most honest and decent women that I know. I didn't know her mother or her sister, but I can't imagine them being anything but decent women as well. I'm not about to sit here and listen to you talk down to a woman that I consider to be the best friend that I've ever had." Sister Emmagene exploded.

"Aah, best friends? How sweet. The black widow and the daughter of the hoe." Lula Mae smiled. "Maybe the two of you can open a brothel."

"How dare you? I'm nobody's black widow," Sister Emmagene cried before running out of the hospital room.

"Weak little women want to do war with mama cat, how pathetic," Lula Mae giggled.

Aunt HoneyBea stood stone-faced while slowly walking closer to Lula Mae's bed. She gripped the breathing tube with her right hand and squeezed tightly. Lula Mae's eyes grew to be as round as golf balls. She gasped for air while wailing her frail arms to fight off my aunt, but she was too weak. Aunt HoneyBea's grasp on the tube continued to tighten.

"You listen to me, you old wart. You sit back here and act all 'holier-than-thou' with those who are dumb enough to believe you, but I know better. You are just a scared old woman who believes someone better is coming to take what you never deserved. My mother never wanted your husband and you know it, but your insecurities sure led you to believe that he wanted her. I always thought you were strong. I even modeled my own life after that image, but now I truly see you for who you are. You're insecure, wicked, and weak. Tell me where I can find my niece or die at the hands of an Arden woman. Die beneath me like the snake that you have always been." Aunt HoneyBea looked upon Lula Mae with a stare that screamed murder.

"You won't kill me. You can't do it." Lula Mae struggled to speak while gasping for air.

"Like you said, you're dying anyway. I'm just speeding up the process," Aunt HoneyBea said.

"Okay, let go of the damn tube," Lula Mae incoherently coughed, but Aunt HoneyBea understood her. She loosened her grip on the tube just enough for Lula Mae to continue speaking. "If I know my son, he took her to the old plantation house, just outside of town."

"Thank you," Aunt HoneyBea said before releasing the breathing tube all together.

"Don't thank me. I chose that daughter-in-law of mine very well. She is strong in all the ways that my son is weak. She's the perfect kitten to step up to the mantle of mama cat. I'm sure your niece is already dead." Lula Mae coughed while continuing to pant for air.

"And if she is, you'd better believe that I'm coming back to send your old behind back to hell where you belong," Aunt HoneyBea said before walking out into the hallway to face a teary-eyed Sister Emmagene.

"You must think I'm some sort of monster," Sister Emmagene wept.

"Emmagene, this is Hurley. All people do around these parts is gossip all day. By your second day here, the death of your husband was already local chatter. I don't pay any attention to that trash. I judge your character by the character that you show me, and honey you are one of the best friends that I have. You annoy my nerves to no end, but I love you, girl."

"Oh my God, Beatrice, I don't know what to say." Sister Emmagene beamed with happiness.

"Chile, don't say anything. Just get me to a phone so I can call Darryl Junior. I know where to find my Rumor." Aunt HoneyBea smiled. Even with everything that had occurred, her faith was still strong. Deep inside, she knew that my heart was still beating.

Rumor's Journal (Entry 13)

It takes great faith to break the snake,
That venomous beast of yesterday.
Those sleeping dogs will never wake.
Bygones be bygones it will never say.
It holds envy close like the best of friends,
Because in the end, it would rather
die than let the righteous win.

Chapter 14

The Cat's Vendetta

Mixing love and lies left Aunt HoneyBea ridden with overwhelming amounts of guilt. She found that lying to yourself to protect the object of your romantic love was never a good idea. The outcome left her with blood-stained hands that only the grace of God could clean. Chrisette, on the other hand, had not yet seen such consequences. She was still trapped in the center of a battle between her true love for Darryl Junior and her own misguided pride. She wanted to be honest with him. Her desire to submit to her emotions had hit an all-time peak, but her fear of heartache was a barrier she had not yet overcome.

Chrisette sat quietly in the passenger seat of Deputy Ron's police cruiser as he trailed Sheriff Mack through the downtrodden slums of Mercy Projects. Darryl Junior and Funyun rode along with Sheriff Mack in the other vehicle. They were following up on an anonymous tip that I had been spotted in the housing development. Throughout the majority of the trip Chrisette had not spoken one word. Her mind was possessed by thoughts of Darryl Junior. It was only a few hours ago that she feared his life had been lost to Caesar Grimes' dastardly plans. The thought of permanently losing Darryl Junior had provided her feelings of desperation and pain that she never thought to be possible.

"You really love him, don't you?" Deputy Ron glanced over at Chrisette who had not once removed her stare from Darryl Junior in the car ahead of them.

"Excuse me! Do I know you?" Chrisette rolled her eyes before shifting her sights to the view outside of the passenger side window.

"It's cool if you don't wanna talk about it, but I can't help but notice how quiet you are. Obviously something is on your mind."

"I'm just tired. I've had a long past couple of days." Chrisette sighed.

"Yea, I can imagine. I know you didn't show up for us, but regardless I never got a chance to thank you before. If you had not shown up when you did, there's no telling what me and my lil' brother would have done to each other." Deputy Ron contemplated back on the look of hatred that burned from his brother's face the night before.

"What's up with that anyway? You and Gia? She's only 16 years old." Chrisette turned a condescending eye towards the deputy.

"I wish I knew. I hate that I feel the way that I do for her. I really do, but I can't stop thinking about Gia. My brother and I were never really close. We're way too different, but I never thought that I would hurt him like this. I wish I could take it all back, but I'm scared that even if I did, I'd just fall in love with her all over again."

"Wow. That's real. Although I don't approve of a 23 year old man being with a 16 year old girl, I do understand the struggle of not controlling who you love. I've tried so hard to get over Darryl Junior, but I just can't get him off my mind. This last time was the closest I've ever come to moving on. I had convinced myself that we were better off being apart, but when I overheard Red's plan with Caesar, Darryl was the only thing on my mind. If something ever happened to him . . ." Chrisette paused.

"What? If something ever happened to him, what?" Deputy Ron asked.

Chrisette looked forward at Darryl Junior sitting in the passenger seat of Sheriff Mack's car. With the love of her life as a fixture within her heart, she opened her mouth preparing to finish her statement when Sheriff Mack's car suddenly spun out of control. Chrisette screamed, "Darryl."

Deputy Ron smashed against the car's break as steel spikes came into view on the road beneath them. Sheriff's Mack's cruiser continued to spin wildly across lanes then flipped twice before roughly landing upside down against a blacktop parking lot. Chrisette watched in disbelief as the car burst into flames. Her greatest fear was becoming a reality before her very eyes. She couldn't move or speak. The terror of the moment had left her completely paralyzed.

Deputy Ron raced to his father's car and yanked against the jammed driver's side door. The flames grew wild against the heat of the black-top pavement. Sheriff Mack was bleeding from his forehead, but the impact of the crash had not knocked him unconscious. Darryl Junior and Funyun, on the other hand, were both out cold as the flames proceeded to envelop the vehicle. With Deputy Ron pulling against the jammed door and his father pushing from the other side, the door eventually gave way and released the sheriff from its fiery hold.

"Dad, you okay?" Deputy Ron shouted with relief.

"I'm fine. Don't worry about me. Let's get the fellas out," Sheriff Mack replied.

Chrisette was still frozen in time as the chaotic scene developed before her very eyes. She could see and hear everything, but somehow her mind was lost in a trance. She envisioned a long, flowing white dress, and a genuine smile as it formed across her face. She could see Darryl Junior in a tuxedo. As he smiled, there was a light in his eyes that she hadn't seen since their days as a couple. Everyone clapped and cheered around them as they grasped each other's hands. The platinum bands of their wedding rings clasped in unison. It was a brief vision but also a moment of pure emotional ecstasy for Chrisette. She awakened from her day dream just in time to hear Darryl Junior shout in panic. He had awakened to face the hot flames that were quickly gaining on him.

Chrisette immediately regained her senses and jumped from the car. Both the Sheriff and Deputy were struggling to help Darryl Junior out of his safety belt and at the same time trying to keep him calm. Darryl Junior yanked wildly against the belt making it difficult for either of them to reach it. At the sound of Darryl's screams, Funyun slowly regained consciousness as well. He also panicked. Chrisette ran to face Darryl Junior.

"Chrisette, get back!" Sheriff Mack warned.

"No, dad. Let her talk to him. She can calm him down." Deputy Ron knew the connection that Chrisette and Darryl shared all too well. He shared a similar connection with Gia. He could remember the chaos of the day that Manny kidnapped Gia. Even then, he knew that nothing or no one would ever keep him from her, and knowing that, he wouldn't dare stand in between Darryl Junior and Chrisette in their moment of crisis.

"Darryl, it's me, baby. It's Chrissy. I'm here. Just calm down and let the officers help you. We're going to get you out of there, baby. Just hold tight. I won't let you die. I love you too much to ever let you go again." Chrisette cried.

"Okay baby. Okay. I love you too, Chrissy. I love you too," Darryl Junior said as he sat calmly focusing on Chrisette's beautiful face. Within moments, Sheriff Mack was able to loosen his seat belt and Deputy Ron pulled him free of the car.

As the Sheriff and Deputy pulled Funyun from the back seat, Darryl Junior found himself safe within Chrisette's loving embrace. Even in the midst of a fiery disaster, she still smelled of expensive perfume and essential oils. He found comfort in her presence. "Damn, I love you, girl."

"I know it. Marry me." Chrisette had not even thought of the words as they quickly left her mouth. She spoke out of instinct, but her heart meant every word.

"What did you just say?" Darryl Junior asked.

"Be my husband, Darryl. I don't want to miss you for another moment. Please marry me," Chrissy said.

"Hell yeah! He'll marry you!" just as soon as he was able to free his lungs of the fire fueled smoke, Funyun shouted with excitement.

"What he said." Darryl Junior smiled before giving Chrisette one of the longest and most passionate kisses he could muster. In her mind, Chrisette could still hear the clasping of the wedding bands from her brief vision.

Darryl Junior and Chrisette's engagement was quickly interrupted by a loud ruffle which sounded from a patch of nearby bushes. Funyun was the only one of them to spot the back of a little girl as she quickly dashed inside of an apartment. The five of them ran to the apartment door hoping that the little girl was me or at the least someone who knew of my whereabouts. Sheriff Mack banged loudly against the door with his fists. No one answered. Then Darryl Junior grew impatient and kicked the raggedy door with all of his might.

"Darryl, chill! You can't go around destroying people's property," Deputy Ron said.

"Why are you talking to me, you damn pedophile? Don't get it confused. Just because I'm focused on saving my cousin right now, doesn't mean I forgot what you did to my sister," Darryl snapped.

"Darryl, he just saved your life," Chrisette interjected.

"Don't worry about it, Chrissy. I understand how he feels," Deputy Ron said.

"Man, forget you," Darryl Junior continued.

"Can you all shut up?" Sheriff Mack demanded. His ear was pressed firmly against the door. He could hear footsteps on the other side. "This is Sheriff Ronald Mack. I'm here to follow up on a tip in response to an Amber alert. Please open the door now." Still no one answered.

"That's their second notice, Pops," Deputy Ron said.

"Okay. Let's kick it in," Sheriff Mack said.

Within moments, the door was knocked free of its hinges. The impact sent a cloud of splinters and dust into the apartment. That day's sunlight ruptured through the cloud of ruin revealing both Sheriff and Deputy Mack to the interior scene of the apartment. The carpet was filthy with dirt and aged blood stains. Dirty laundry covered the floor, along with opened containers of molded foods. The television sounded loudly with the sounds of hip hop music videos. Even more so than the filth and loud music, the putrid smell that permeated through the apartment made for virtually unlivable conditions.

Darryl Junior, Chrisette, and Funyun followed the officers with their hands tightly clasped around their noses.

"It smells like straight up ass and frito lay in this spot, bruh." Funyun frowned beneath the pressure of the overwhelming stench.

"Please shut up," Chrisette said.

"Rumor. Rumor, are you in here?" Darryl Junior shouted.

"You three stay back while we check out the place, okay?" Sheriff Mack said as he and his son stepped deeper into the apartment.

"No, I'm coming . . . Ouch." Darryl Junior attempted to object until Chrisette sharply nudged his ribs with her elbow.

"Yes sir. No problem," Chrisette said while cutting her eyes at her new fiancé.

Sheriff Mack proceeded into the hallway of the unkempt apartment. Deputy Ron followed closely, watching his father's back as they trekked into unfamiliar territory. At the end of the hallway they could hear the sound of running water coming from the bathroom. The door was slightly cracked. Sheriff Mack slowly pushed it open. They were both surprised to find that no one was there. The floor was soaked with water from the overflowing bathtub. Sheriff Mack leapt across the water and turned off the shower. Just as Deputy Ron stepped inside of the bathroom as well, the door quickly shut behind them. They both quickly turned to take sight of a short assailant covered with a black hoodie and a vampire Halloween mask. Water splashed across the floor as the hood-wearing assailant leapt from the top of the door frame. Deputy Ron reached for his billy club as quickly as possible, but he was not able to reach it before he was bum rushed by the tiny attacker. Deputy Ron fell backwards knocking Sheriff Mack into the bathtub full of water. The masked assailant proceeded to pound Deputy Ron with his fists. Deputy Ron shielded his face and yanked the Halloween mask from his attacker's face.

As Deputy Ron took sight of his attacker, the bathroom door swung open. "Sheriff. Deputy. You guys have gotta see this," Chrisette exclaimed.

Deputy Ron's attacker froze giving him adequate enough time to push the person away. "Tasha Tahiri?" Sheriff Mack dripped with water as he stood to take sight of one third of the Tahiri triplets.

"Ay man, get off my sister." Tamika Tahiri ran from behind Chrisette as the remaining sister, Tami, followed her.

"What's going on here? You girls had better start talking now," Deputy Ron yelled.

"We found something in the bedroom that should explain a lot," Chrisette chimed in.

What they found in the bedroom was enough to give them all the creeps. Lying on an old, ragged mattress in the center of the floor was an extremely frail and sickly Tavis Tahiri. In the middle of the warm, musty room, Tavis shivered as if he were in the midst of the Antarctic. Deep, dark circles enclosed around his eyes. His arms were filled with a countless number of injection scars.

"This is impossible. My department found this man dead days ago." Sheriff Mack took a closer look of the downtrodden drug addict.

"I-i-it's me Sheriff." Tavis stuttered.

"Don't touch my brother. I ain't scared of no po—po." Tasha Tahiri raced to her brother's side.

"Young lady, we're the police. We're here to help. Why didn't you tell us your brother was alive?" Sheriff Mack knelt down to face Tasha.

"Don't talk down to me, po po. I ain't no dummy. Ya'll tried to kill my brother. Tami saw the whole thing," Tasha continued.

"We tried to kill him?" Deputy Ron asked.

"It wasn't them, Tasha; but they were police. It was four of 'em. They shot him up with a bunch of crack needles," Tami said.

"This doesn't make any sense," Sheriff Mack said.

"It makes plenty sense to me, Sheriff. It sounds like Caesar's corrupted a few of your men," Darryl Junior said.

"N-n-no. Not C-c-ceasar. V Gatto." Tavis struggled to speak.

"Did you just say V Gatto?" Darryl Junior asked.

"Yeah. He been sayin' that name since we found him. Who is that chick, anyway?" Tasha asked.

"Yeah, Darryl. Who the hell is that?" Chrisette questioned.

"I mean I don't know much about her. She's kind of a legend in Biloxi. I just always assumed she was some old country urban legend or some thug fairy tale meant to scare people. They say she ran New York for years as a black queen of organized crime. Supposedly the Feds got wind of her operations so she moved her empire to Biloxi where she started running a brothel. I've never seen the woman, myself," Darryl Junior explained.

"S-she's real. She's h-here," Tavis said.

"Ron, radio the station and ask for Deputy Terry. Don't talk to anyone but Terry. I trust that man with my life. Ask him to pull up a rap sheet for a V Gatto," Sheriff Mack ordered.

"Yes, Sir," Deputy Ron answered before racing out to his police car.

It wasn't long before Deputy Terry located the FBI criminal file of Vendetta D Gatto, better known as V Gatto. Her name was Italian. It was borrowed from her roots within the Italian mafia where she learned skills which allowed her to produce her own underground cartel of criminal activity. Its meaning can be loosely translated into the Cat's Revenge. After her disappearance from New York in the early 1950s, V Gatto rose to power again many years later as the owner of a Biloxi brothel. Her girls serviced very rich and powerful men within the southern community. V Gatto extorted and blackmailed many of these men to solidify her return to criminal dominance. She was an expert as she never left behind prosecutable evidence. The only thing the Federal Investigators could ever find were black diamonds which were cut to resemble the head of a cat. Eventually, the FBI was again hot on her trail, but she soon disappeared. The female crime lord was never heard of again outside of gossip and rumor until recently. After calling in to the FBI, Terry found that my mother, Alieza Arden, had stumbled upon evidence of V Gatto's operations. As an undercover informant, Alieza worked as an escort under the supervision of Caesar Grimes who was believed to be the decoy leader for V Gatto's continued operations. She served the FBI with every piece of information that she could find until her recent and untimely death.

As the newest and hottest drug dealer on the blocks of Mercy Projects, Tavis Tahiry was seen as a minor roadblock to V Gatto's growing operations. She ordered a hit on his life. Knowing that Caesar Grimes was on his way to ensure that the job was completed, Alieza tried to warn Tavis of the hit. She was, however, distracted while trying to find me during Hurricane Veronya's rampage. Five of Hurley's finest police officers were bribed to carry out the hit. On that day as the rest of the town was distracted by Veronya, Tavis was forcefully injected with enough cocaine to fly an elephant.

Within an hour, paramedics arrived on the scene with stretchers to escort Tavis to the hospital. The majority of Sheriff Mack's office entered the crime scene as well. Sheriff Mack had already asked Tami Tahiry to describe the officers who attacked her brother. Just as he was preparing to confront his department's traitors, he was blocked by none other than Old Man Pete.

"Pete? What are you doing here?" Sheriff Mack asked.

"I know what you're about to do, Sheriff; but I can assure you that that would not be a smart move. If we're going to bring down V Gatto and save that little girl, we have to keep everything on the down low for now." Old Man Pete spoke differently than anyone was used to him speaking. His backwoods, country dialect was not nearly as heavy as usual. His words were complete and clearly enunciated.

"Pete, what do you know about all of this?" Sheriff Mack said.

"I'm Special Investigator James Benson. Peter is my middle name. I went undercover 20 years ago trying to track Gatto. I became so obsessed with the case that I was fired from the Bureau, but I continued to track Vendetta here in Hurley on my own ever since."

"Is this some kind of joke?" Sheriff Mack's facial expression grew tight with confusion.

"I wish it were," Old Man Pete said before throwing his arm around Sheriff Mack and ushering him away from the possibility of prying ears.

"Why wasn't I informed about this? This is my county. Where does the FBI get off sneaking around my county?" Sheriff Mack complained.

"As you now see for yourself, Sheriff, I couldn't trust that your department had not been compromised. Gatto is a very crafty woman. She's done this many times before. I had to be smart about this investigation."

"If she's been in Hurley for the past twenty years, who is she?" Sheriff Mack asked. "I know every single citizen of this town."

"I said I've been investigating her for twenty years. She's been here for much longer," Old Man Pete said. "We knew that she had to be hiding in some sort of small town in order for her to fly so low beneath our radar. After studying small counties near Biloxi, Hurley was the obvious choice. After a few years of observing this town I almost gave up on the investigation. That was until the night that I ran into Alieza Arden. It was a rainy night about 13 years ago. The poor girl was drenched and terrified. I knew from the look in her eyes that whatever she had witnessed could not have been normal for this quiet little town. From working as a janitor in the school, I'd gained a certain amount of rapport with Ms. Arden. She confided in me."

"So what did she see?"

"She saw her then boyfriend, Bernard Johnson, beat within an inch of his life by his own mother. She said Lula Mae had caught them in her basement having relations. Bernard hid Alieza behind a stack of boxes, but Alieza could still see Lula Mae as she lost control."

"Lula Mae beat Pastor Bernard, but we arrested Caesar for that beating?" Sheriff Mack said. "What does this have to do with V Gatto?"

"Lula Mae lost control of her senses as she beat the boy. She screamed all sorts of strange obscenities, but it was one thing that Alieza heard that grabbed my interest. Lula Mae kept referring to herself as Mama Cat. Mama Cat was the code name V Gatto used to covertly carry out her operations when she ran the boroughs of New York."

"Lula Mae Johnson? You've got to be kidding me."

"Again Sheriff, I wish I were," Old Man Pete said.

Sheriff Mack was lost in disbelief. How could all of this have occurred right beneath his nose for so many years without him knowing? Lula Mae had long been a staple within Hurley's high society. Behind the scenes, it was she who truly ran the church. He often noticed that she was a tyrant in the way that she commanded respect from the people of Hurley. Her methods were very often excessive but they were effective. Looking back on it all, they were methods she had clearly learned from her decades of hustling the streets. Lula Mae was V Gatto.

"Sheriff Mack." Darryl Junior came running up behind them both. "I just got a call from my Aunt HoneyBea. Rumor is at the Johnson's old plantation just outside of town, and Caesar may be there with Silvia Johnson. Apparently, they're in on this together."

"How does she know all this?" Old Man Pete asked. Sheriff Mack was still too full of surprise to speak.

"She says she talked to Lula Mae Johnson," Darryl Junior answered. Upon hearing her name, both Sheriff Mack and Old Man Pete quickly jumped to action.

Rumor's Journal (Entry 14)

A lie can be living, breathing flesh,
Wrapped in a façade of what the holy confess,
Self-righteous kings and queens of the lost,
Of all that is grimy and mean, she is boss.
Right beneath your nose, she lives amongst you,
Like a cat hair she flows within and infects you.
Remember, adapt and uphold this motto.
Never enter the path of the one known as Gatto.

Chapter 15

Last Words

As my family scrambled to find me, I hid quietly away in the confines of the Johnson family's dark, murky basement. In the silence of my own fear, every little noise stood out within my mind. There was the slow drip of the old, leaky pipes. The tip toe of tiny rat feet against the decaying wood floors sounded like the cadence of an entire military. Floor boards creaked for no apparent reason. Other miscellaneous sounds that I could not identify also haunted my ears to no end. This must have been the terror that Lucky felt. Noises were closing in all around me and there was no way for me to identify if they were the ones which meant me harm.

My nerves felt as if they were about to explode. I struggled to contain my trembling body and prevent it from setting off any detectable noises. I closed my eyes and searched for happy thoughts. Ever since Gia had dropped the bomb of truth on me, my mind had been bombarded with so much negativity. At first, it was hard to find even one happy thought. That was until I spotted the dusty merry-go-round on the other side of the room. In my thoughts, it lit up just as beautifully as it had the night that my mother and Lucky last rode it. Music filled the room as the merry-go-round spun freely on its axis. After that, the dam of negativity was broken. Happy thoughts flowed through my mind like the waters of the Mississippi river. I could see my Aunt Mildred both laughing and playing with me. Her many ailments no longer restricted her. If anything, they gave her visions of wonder. Through her eyes, I was Alieza. She hugged me tightly, and through her I could feel a love that my mother undoubtedly enjoyed. Then there was the grassy field of butterflies. Elaborately colored wings filled the sky. They filled the sky so deeply that the Mississippi sun could only shine through their colors. Gorgeous shades of lavender, yellow, bright blue, pink, orange and more filled the grassy lands below. It was an unbelievable sight as Taylor and I basked in the center of the surreal landscape of beauty.

Then last but not least, there was my mother. She stood tall and beautiful just as I last remembered her. The Mississippi sun cast a direct spotlight across her. She danced and sang as the tail of her long sun dress flowed behind her. There was peace and tranquility in her smile. It was a peace and tranquility that conflicted with the many stories of pain and turmoil that I had recently discovered. It was the same peace that I had chosen to remember for so many years. Looking upon her, I finally realized that no matter what they had done to Alieza Arden, she was able to maintain some level of purity. She maintained just enough beauty and innocence to pass down to me. Their dark lies had not destroyed her, but it was her own white lies that maintained her. She maintained herself through the mask of perfection that she had worn in order to preserve me. Despite everything, my mother was an angel. Whether in life or in death, she lived every day of her existence as my guardian angel.

The knock of hard bottom shoes against the creaking wood floors pulled me away from my happy thoughts. The footsteps grew louder as their owner descended deeper into the basement. I laid back behind the stack of boxes which hid me and closed my eyes.

"Little girl, don't be afraid. Caesar's not going to hurt you. You know I have a daughter of my own. In fact, I believe you're best friends with my grandson. Do you think that I would do anything to upset my only grandchild? Just come out and talk to old Caesar." Caesar Grimes walked slowly while attempting to play upon my intelligence.

"The chiles no fool, but Tuna feels she is close," Miss Tuna said to Caesar.

"Well you better turn up that mambo juice and find her. I'm not paying you for the hell of it," Caesar said.

"Calm down, Missa Grimes. Tuna deliver on her promise. Tuna give Missa Grimes all secrets she collect from the faithless people of Hurley."

"Those secrets mean nothing if this lil girls gets away and exposes my plans. The church is desperate and the people have lost faith in their leaders, but if they find out I orchestrated Pastor Bernard, Sheriff Mack and Mayor Clarke's downfalls, they will never trust me to be their new leader," Caesar Grimes complained.

"No worries, Missa Grimes. Tuna gon' handle this . . ." Miss Tuna turned to Caesar with reassuring eyes that quickly fell weak behind the sound of a muffled gun shot.

Caesar turned to track the source of the gun shot to First Lady Silvia Johnson. "Silvia, what the hell are you doing?"

"You men are so foolish. I am past tired of that old woman and your superstitious belief in her so-called magic. She was nothing more than an informant. A pawn in V Gatto's plans, just like you." Silvia confidently spoke with her gun now aimed at Caesar's head.

"What do you know about V Gatto?" Caesar asked.

"Apparently a lot more than you. You really should make it your business to get to know your employer," Silvia said.

"No one knows V Gatto. The woman is a ghost," Caesar said.

"Really? A ghost. How cute," Silvia said before reaching down into her blouse and pulling out a necklace with a small, black cat diamond hanging from it. "Do you know the greatest lie that the devil ever told mankind?"

"Silvia, what the hell are you talking about? Put that gun down?" Caesar attempted to grab the gun from Silvia's grip, but not before she set off a round of bullets at his feet.

"Uh. Uh. Uh. I wouldn't do that if I were you. Now answer the question." Silvia smiled.

"I don't know, woman. What's the greatest lie the devil ever told?"

"He made you fools believe that he didn't exist." Silvia laughed before sending a bullet clean through Caesar's cranium. Caesar fell down the stairs and died instantly.

"The mantle of the cat lives on through me. This is why they'll never catch us. V Gatto was never just one woman. V Gatto is a torch that has now been passed on to me, and nobody is going to stop me from carrying out Lula Mae's vendetta. And that means you, Rumor." Silvia said before randomly shooting a bullet off into the basement.

"You see, I know you hear me little girl. I've been waiting a long time for this moment. You have no idea what it was like being married to that weak little man. Always talking about Rumor this and Rumor that. Girl, please. You are the child of a slut. Everyone thinks that you are so special. I never could understand why." Silvia spoke while searching through the basement.

"I mean don't misunderstand me, this is far from personal. I don't care enough about you to hate you, Rumor, but Lula Mae always saw you as a threat to our power. I mean you are the illegitimate child of the face of our church. We can't have that little bit of information leaking, now can we? So you see it's all business. You have to die. Being V Gatto is all about power, honey. What's more powerful than the church? I mean really, drug cartels are nice but a man's faith controls him a lot more than any drug ever could. Nothing is going to stand in between me and that power. Not even a twelve-year-old little girl."

Listening to her as she rambled on, I couldn't take it anymore. Lula Mae was responsible for everything that had happened to my mother. Her stupid vendetta had cost my entire family a grave price. I had no idea what this V Gatto that she kept referring to was, but I knew that I was done hiding from it. I crept out from behind the boxes and stood to face her.

"Perfect. Caesar killed my husband, the old conjure woman, and you. I got here just in time to stop him. How sad that I couldn't save you first, but oh well, the world will move on." Silvia aimed the gun straight for my head.

"Before you pull that trigger, I just wanna tell you one last thing," I said.

"Hurry up, little girl. I don't have all day," Silvia said.

"Watch your step." I smiled. Silvia didn't realize it but she was standing on top of the merry-go-round. The plug was not far from where I hid. I put it into the outlet before I came out of hiding. I had no idea whether it would work or not, but I was willing to bet my life on it. I flipped the switch, sending power through the outlet and into the merry-go-round. Silvia looked confused at first, but then she quickly shook it off before tightening her grip on the gun's trigger. Just as the bullet prepared to release, the merry-go-round sparked and shifted beneath her. Silvia was caught off guard by the sudden movement and the bright light. She fell onto her back sending the bullet upwards into the ceiling. Quickly I pounced on her causing her to lose her grip on the pistol. The weapon fell to the ground as she and I tussled aboard the spinning merry-go-round.

"Get off of me," Silvia screamed while pushing me backwards with all of her strength. She climbed on top of me and balled her hand into a tight first. "I guess I'll just have to kill you with my own damn hands then."

"Over my dead body." A bloody and weakened Pastor Bernard appeared with Silvia's gun in his hands.

"Bernard, honey, what are you doing? We both know you're not going to kill me. I'm your wife." Silvia looked up with a fake smile.

"I should've protected Alieza from you, Mama. I was too weak to protect the woman that I loved, but I will do anything to protect our daughter." Pastor Bernard cried.

"Bernard, I'm not your mother. It's me, Silvia."

"Get off her, Mother." Pastor Bernard shouted before shooting Silvia directly in her chest. She fell backwards and was flung by the momentum of the merry-go-round onto the floor. The black cat diamond from her necklace rolled onto the floor beside her. It was covered with enough blood to mark the end of V Gatto's reign.

"Pastor Bernard, are you okay." I jumped from the merry-go-round as he collapsed onto the ground as well. I pulled him into my arms. He was bleeding profusely. I had no idea how to save him.

"Rumor, baby, I'm your father. I'm your father." Those were his last words.

Rumor's Journal (Entry 15)

I thought death was the end,
But at the point of loss, my life began.
New worlds opened as seasons transcend,
Opportunities bloomed from the God within,
Now I hear the whispers of the wind,
They say you shall survive, my friend.

Chapter 16

Our Story

Crushed berry colors shone beneath the light of day. A wall that had for so long been lost to shadows was now unveiled for the entire city to see. My mother's mural seemed even more amazing as everyone in Hurley gazed on its story. It told a captivating story that captured the eyes of everyone. It was a story that none of them knew. It was her story. It was my story, and on that Sunday morning, it became Pastor Bernard's story as well.

Painting was never my talent, but my father was no shadow. He was a great man, a man of color. I'd watched him in his last moment. I took witness of the brown color in his eyes as they expanded into royal blue, green, and yellow shades of splendor. Those were the colors of his soul. After I squished bundles of berries within the palms of my hands, I ran them across the mural's shadow man. The rough wall melted into a creamy smoothness beneath the pressure of my fingers. I wiped the berries until they merged into various colors. Eventually, the art took a life of its own. It was almost as if there were more than two hands against the wall. There were four. My mother had joined me to finish the painting she had so long ago started, and within seconds, our story was complete. The truth was loud and colorful against the church wall. The truth would never again be ignored. We were a family, and I was the product of light, beauty and sheer splendor.

Months had passed since my father's death. At first there was a sadness that grew within the city. It was an incurable depression that consumed every living thought. Our city's leader had died, and just like his ashes, his energy had left us with the blowing wind. Hurley seemed hopeless, until the day that Deacon Booker walked to the front step of my auntie's porch. Deputy Mayor Owen, who was now running the city during the Mayor's absence, stood by his side.

"Rumor, Deacon Booker is here to see you," Aunt HoneyBea shouted.

As I raced to the front door, I wasn't surprised to see them there. Many people had visited over those last weeks with their condolences, but I was surprised to see the look of happiness glowing across the Deacon's face. His smile seemed genuine. It was nothing like the many forced smiles that I had become so accustomed to seeing.

"How's it going, Deacon?" I asked.

"Good Afternoon, Rumor! It's such a blessing to see that you are holding up well. You are such a strong little girl. That's definitely something that you get from your father," Deacon Booker said.

"She got it honestly from both her parents," Aunt HoneyBea grinned.

"Thanks, Deacon," I said with my eyes locked on the ground beneath me.

"Well, I guess you ladies are wondering why Ms. Owen and I are here," Deacon Booker said. "A lot has happened over the past couple of months. I've tried to reignite the fire within this community, but I just can't seem to do it. Pastor Bernard had a way of touching people. I can't replace that."

"Oh Deacon, I'm sure you'll do fine. You give great sermons," Aunt HoneyBea said.

"He does, but it's going to take more than a great sermon to reach the people of Hurley. Their spirits have been crushed, Ms. HoneyBea."

"What does any of this have to do with my Rumor?" Aunt HoneyBea asked.

"I'm glad you asked. While going through the church yesterday, we came across an old mural," Deacon Booker said.

"My mama's mural?" I asked excitedly.

"Yes, your mama's mural. Rumor, I'd like you to finish that mural. We want to unveil it to the church on Sunday. Paint your father and show the world his light," Deacon Booker proclaimed.

"Oh Deacon, Rumor doesn't paint," Aunt HoneyBea said.

"No, Auntie, I'll do it. I'll do it for my mama." I smiled. My mother must have heard me that day, because I know that her soul found me as I painted that wall. It was her gift to me and my gift to Hurley.

My family was proud of me as we all watched the wall. Aunt HoneyBea never took her eyes off of me as the church shouted and praised God with joy. Darryl Junior and Chrisette both gripped my shoulders to express their approval and pride. Even Gia winked at me on the sly. It was a glorious moment. It was my mother's redemption. As a young girl, she was rejected by this town, but on that day, it was clear that she would forever be honored by their admiration.

She and my father were finally together in heaven. Later that afternoon Aunt HoneyBea cooked one of her famous dinners. Her crispy fried chicken, macaroni and cheese, barbecued meats, baked beans, collard greens, deviled eggs, and her famous peach cobbler filled the air with the smell of love. The entire town gathered on the grassy field of butterflies. We ate, laughed, and fellowshipped like the family that we were.

Deputy Mayor Owen commanded everyone's attention for an amazing announcement. The FBI had donated the black cat diamonds recovered from the investigation of V Gatto to the rebuilding fund of our hurricane damaged city. It was a moment of pure elation as everyone shouted and yelled with joy. I looked around at all of their smiling faces, and I had never been more proud to call Hurley my home.

Even Gia smiled as she exchanged occasional glances with Deputy Mack. Out of concern for appearances, they dared not speak, but there was an unspoken love that still burned within the both of them. Only God knew whether there would be a future for the two of them as a couple, but in that moment, they were both clearly content in knowing that the other was happy.

Taylor's injuries had fully healed. He was starting to change right before my eyes. His voice was a lot deeper. He'd experienced a growth spurt that ended with him being the tallest guy in our class. Despite all of the change that we'd both experienced, our friendship remained the same. Hand in hand, we laughed as the afternoon winds rushed past us. The high grass of the fields slapped against our bodies. Hundreds of colorful butterflies flew beside us. It felt great as we once again found ourselves flying with the butterflies. With pride, I looked ahead into the eyes of the bright sun eager to continue my journey into womanhood.

I am Rumor Arden and now you know my story. May God bless every eye that glances upon these words. Hopefully they will prove to be just as much of a blessing to those who will read them as they were to me as I wrote them.

ABOUT THE AUTHOR

J.E. Tyler is an author, poet, and entrepreneur determined to find success as a published fiction author. It is the realization of this dream that motivated Tyler to found his publishing company, Zodiac Gifted Publishing also known as ZOGI Publishing. Through this imprint, Tyler has self-published the dramatic science fiction novel **REG Aftermath** and the spiritually inspiring and dramatic novel **Rumor: Daughter of Lies.** Tyler has written stage play productions for his hometown church,

Destiny Vision Christian Center. He is also the author of the well-reviewed short stories, **The Girl Who Stole From Fire** and **That Dance That We Do.** Tyler obtained a Bachelors of Science in Business Management from Alabama A and M University, where he crossed the burning sands of Alpha Phi Alpha Fraternity, Incorporated. He also has a Master's of Business Administration from Texas A and M University. Look for this young man to utilize his God given talents and well-educated business acumen to dominate the book publishing industry and more in the future.

Please feel free to email Tyler with any questions regarding his past, current, or upcoming novels. Your feedback is greatly appreciated.

Jtyler1985@live.com
www.facebook.com/ZOGI.media

Made in the USA
San Bernardino, CA
17 April 2014